DEATH BY CHOCOLATE

by Emma Walker

Emma Walker

First Edition

Copyright © Emma Walker 2007

The right of Emma Walker to be identified as the Author of the Work has been asserted by her in accordance with the Copyright, Designs and Patents Act 1988.

All rights reserved. No part of this publication may be reproduced, stored in a retrieval system, or transmitted, in any form or by any means without the prior written permission of the author, nor be otherwise circulated in any form of binding or cover other than that in which it is published and without similar condition being imposed on the subsequent purchaser.

Cover artwork by Drin Chulakasyena. (Additional colouring by Christopher Chamberlain.)

All characters in this publication are fictitious and any resemblance to real persons, living or dead, is purely coincidental.

ISBN: 978-0-9559788-0-7

Printed and bound by Lulu. Published by M Publications.

Death By Chocolate

Contents

	Page
Sleep Safety	6
Making An Appointment	12
Add Vices (Part 1)	21
Interlude: The Devil Came For Georgia	24
Add Vices (Part 2)	27
The Stars In The Night Sky	32
Caution	34
Bring Out Your Dead	37
The Court Of Angels	42
Confessions Of A Loser	48
Sinner Man	51
The Investigation	64
Private Investigations	73
The Miracle Cure	84
Mind Tricks	91
Waiting For…	95
Watching The Detectives	99
The First Circle	104
Cloud Eight	108
Back To Life	111
The Deal	118
Avenging Angels	123
Two's A Crowd	125
The Parties	133
Up On The Rooftops	141
Protection	144
Morana's Day	152
Review	170

Alter's Day	177
Morana And Alter Are Recorded In Front Of A Live TV Audience	183
The Last Visit	191
Hell's Angel	201
And In The End...	207
Epilogue	212
Deleted Scenes	216

Death By Chocolate

Emma Walker

Sleep Safety

Alter stood at the end of the bed, wearing the same crumpled black boxer shorts and creased olive green t-shirt with the golden horn motif that he'd worn to bed last night. Not that he'd spent a lot of time in his own bed. He grinned at the sleeping figure of Morana, curled up warmly in her quilt, bathed in the muted sunlight trickling through the thin pink curtains. He loved their morning ritual.

...Try to wake me at 6 a.m. and there's an eighty percent chance you'll cry...

Alter's wide grin somehow extended as he produced a foghorn from somewhere behind his back. He held it aloft, put his other finger in his opposite ear, and let the sound blast across the bedroom, bouncing off the walls around them. After a suitable number of seconds, he slowly lowered both his hands and watched his victim. Morana merely groaned, pulling the quilt tightly over her head.

Alter huffed, but not with defeat. He considered the terrain; then, with renewed determination and grinning, he gently lifted the quilt at the foot of the bed, beached the foghorn just between her feet and pressed the button for a second satisfying blast. Alter pulled out the foghorn and giggled to himself. Morana made no movement or sound at all this time. Undeterred, Alter made for his next move, tiptoeing like a schoolboy to the head of the bed.

Placing the horn quietly onto her bedside table, he cagily peeled the cover away from her sleeping face.

Morana's visage looked up at him, whiter than a sheet of bleached paper, a river of deep red blood seeping slowly out of her nose, vaulting her pursed lips, slithering down her chin, and dripping on to her neck. Alter bounded out of the room with a girlie scream, slamming the door behind him. The noise of which, ironically, finally woke Morana from her deathly deep sleep. Without moving her body, she reached her hand out from beneath the bedcovers and allowed it to fumble blindly about the bedside table, knocking Alter's foghorn to the floor (which tooted briefly with its downfall), until her fingers landed on the softness of a tissue. Without opening her eyes, she brought the occupied hand towards her nose, wiped away the red liquid, and promptly curled over onto her side, drifting dryly back to sleep, the bloodied tissue sticking to her fingers and blowing gently in the breeze of her snoring.

⌛

Yes, Alter loved their morning ritual. Every dawn was a renewed delightful torture. And his victim was always far too impervious and decent to complain. The following morning, Alter once again stood at the end of the bed, wearing the same crumpled black boxers and creased green t-shirt he'd been wearing to bed all week - whenever he'd made it to bed - and planned the morning's tactics. Always with the same mischievous grin, he looked down at the sleeping body.

> *...Try to wake me at 6:30 a.m. and there's an eighty percent chance I'll forgive...*

Taking hold of the quilt beside her feet, he slowly began to fold it into his hands like a concertina. As the final patch of warmth disappeared from her body, Morana began to move. Without opening her eyes, her arms jerked upwards, her hands pressed down hard on the mattress either side of her, elbows sticking out awkwardly, and with a strength that seemed impossible for such a slumbering pile, she slowly and indelicately slid herself up into a seated position, opened her eyes wide and took in a sharp breath, as if inhaling for the very first time.

⏳

Sometime later, Morana stumbled, with a great many yawns, into their shared kitchen. Alter was already sat at the breakfast table - the long heavy-wooden cottage-kitchen type - eating from a plate piled high with cholesterol-inducing food: eggs, bacon, more eggs, tomatoes, mushrooms, a few more eggs (scrambled, fried and poached, naturally), sausages, black pudding (lots of) and a couple of slices of bread (one toasted and one fried) to mop up the leftovers. He was fully dressed in his working suit, and looked a smart and sophisticated sight to the unknowing.

"Morning, sleepy-head," he greeted Morana. She responded with another yawn, scuffling slowly towards the fridge, opening the door with a scrunch of released air, pulling out a chocolate yoghurt and closing the door behind it with the movements of a mechanical doll. More scuffling followed until she was able to slump into an empty chair opposite her housemate. She thumped the yoghurt pot down on the table and Alter slid a spoon surreptitiously towards her waiting fingers. After a pause for empty thought, Morana began to strip the yoghurt lid away, the seal breaking with a depressing pop.

"Speed kills, you know," Alter remarked, watching her slow work, peeling as if the lid weighed more than she did. Morana ignored his comment, and Alter was unsure if that was deliberate or otherwise. She was more than used to his sarcasm, and he was more than used to her early morning absences.

"What time's your first appointment?" he asked, shovelling another mouthful of fat between his lips. Still as yet unable to bring herself to speak or form suitable word-like shapes with her mouth, Morana wearily reached into her dressing gown pocket and pulled out her PDA. She tapped the button and an appointment appeared on the screen. Barely glimpsing the name, she allowed her eyes to swing towards the time. 7 a.m. Her eyes continued upwards to the clock on the wall beside her. 7:25 a.m. A bolt of adrenaline ran through her body.

"Shh-ugar! God, I'm late!" she yelped.

"Oops," Alter grinned without any sign of surprise. "Probably best you don't tell *Him*," he joked. Morana looked at her housemate with vacant panic in her eyes. "Do you want me to…?" he started to offer, intimating towards her PDA.

"No," she replied, slightly annoyed for the first time that morning. It was just like Alter to pretend he was being helpful by stealing all her appointments. Morana resealed the yoghurt, not yet fully released from its container, scrunching the lip of the lid over the rim in a vain attempt to hold it in place, then got up, returned it to the fridge and walked back towards her bedroom.

"If you're sure...?" Alter called after her nonchalantly, finishing the last of his food with an impish smile. He ran a final chunk of bread around the red, yellow and brown coloured plate, smudging the tones together before popping it into his mouth. Then he dropped the plate into the sink with a clatter and left it to bask in the air.

As he was leaning over to check his reflection in the silvery shine of the toaster, his housemate reappeared with a plastic toothbrush handle sticking out of her mouth. She watched Alter's vanity without open judgement and waited for his own sense of embarrassment to settle in. He stood up sharply and leant against the kitchen counter as coolly as he could, willing her with his eyes to comment. She took the toothbrush out of her mouth and paused.

"But if I'm late, then so are you?" she said, suddenly waking up to the irony, relieved at last to be waking up to something.

"Yep," Alter agreed, flashing her a cocky grin and waddling his head superiorly, "but *I'm* allowed to be." Morana couldn't argue with that. She shrugged with resignation, shoved the toothbrush back into her mouth and returned to the bathroom.

Back on the kitchen table, her PDA bleeped and vibrated alarmingly against the pale wood, the next appointment making its presence known.

Death By Chocolate

"Shh-ugar!" she groaned through a mouthful of bristle and mint. Staring into the bathroom mirror, with toothpaste running down her chin and into the sink below, Morana wondered for a moment what it must be like to be deaf. Her thoughts of such an alternative lifestyle were hastily interrupted by the head of Alter poking around the doorframe. He waved at her to signal his impending departure, and she tried to smile while her gritted teeth tightly gripped the toothbrush.

"Always a pleasure, dear," he said, looking at her splattered nightgown and unkempt hair, which hardly did her already frumpy, dishevelled figure any justice at all. She bent over the sink, spat out the accumulated contents of her mouth, and, in her reflective absence, Alter caught sight of himself in the mirror beaming back handsomely. He smiled appreciatively, running a hand smoothly across his crown, two small horns slowly protruding from his scalp and turning a faint shade of red. "Always a pleasure," he added to his reflection with an approving smile and pointy-hand gesture. Tapping his PDA against the bathroom door to confirm his exit, he left Morana to slowly raise her head and drip in solitude.

"Yeah. Bye," she responded to the click-clunk of the closing front door, a feeling of tired unhappiness washing over her. She returned her toothbrush to the cup on the sink edge, envied its simplistic place in the world, and rubbed at the baggage beneath her eyes. From somewhere just behind her came the same old pulsating bleep.

"Oh, for heaven's sake!" she exploded, her impatience finally rearing.

Emma Walker

Making An Appointment

Morana crept cautiously into the darkened bedroom. The house was empty everywhere else. Today's client didn't appear to have a family, housemate or lodger. Wandering past the living room, bereft of smiling pictures, Morana had felt a pang of sympathy which, like a gust of wind, quickly dissolved behind her as she remembered her job. The only picture in the bedroom hung above the bed, and portrayed an apparently nondescript man on a motorcycle, his identity disguised by a helmet and visor as he and the machine leapt through the air. The gilded frame reflecting the late morning light was of more interest to her. There was a thin, V-shaped crack between the purple curtains letting in the pale sunlight, which bounced upwards through the looping material around the curtain rail, creating a wave imprint against the ceiling. The darkened decor of red walls and dark wood added to the gloom. And there, on the bed, the thin sheets wrapped around its limbs and torso in a less than dignified fashion, was the body. The space surrounding Morana glowed a little more brightly, her simple white dress shimmering with light from an unknown source. Possibly from the two slightly dishevelled, feathery wings now protruding from her spine. She should have looked stylish and grand, but somehow it didn't quite suit her. Her fingers twiddled nervously at the nearest feathers as she began to survey the room, but she was quickly drawn to the man, cowering in the corner, sheltering himself against the bedside table and shivering, wide-eyed with fear. The light increased with her sympathy and she smiled benignly at the quaking face. He watched as the angel's mouth opened, her wings instinctively beginning to spread outwards; an image of supreme grace and ferocious power, he awaited her message with immense trepidation as she announced her entrance with:

"Hello."

His mind went blank as though it were the last part of him to depart the mortal world. No matter how many times she received this vacant response, it still threw her performance. She faltered, her wings curling into themselves.

"Erm... No need to be afraid?"

Still the man shook uncontrollably, but now he began to attempt some movement. One arm slowly lifted from around his knees and protruded outward, parallel to the floor, the index finger of its hand continuing the line across the room. Morana allowed herself to follow the diagonal indication, peaking around the white painted door. Apprehension hit her like a slap to the face. There in the corner, sprawled out comfortably in a dark wicker chair, his knees spread and his fingers tapping gently against the matted wood, sat Alter. His mouth was curled into a cold smile as he watched her recognition. His dark suit sparkled and rippled with a red current, though he sat without obvious movement, avoiding the fall of the natural light. Morana's fingers rippled in a feigned wave.

"You forgot your halo," Alter motioned toward her head. She hurriedly allowed her hands to scramble to her crown and clearly felt the circular halo in place. She scowled at her colleague's mischievous chuckling.

"What are you doing here?"

Alter lifted himself up casually, the chair creaking at the release of weight upon it. He pulled his PDA out of his pocket and met Morana by the door.

"8:45 AM, Mr Michaels," he explained, showing her the details on the screen as he spoke. She looked hard at the details on his machine, internally questioning his honesty, but unable to fault the image. She reached between the folds of her skirt for her own PDA and double checked the appointment, allowing herself a brief moment of doubt in her own abilities to balance out her negative judgment of Alter.

"8:45 AM, Mr Michaels," she reread from her own screen and frowned. She caught Alter's mutual look of confusion, albeit tinged with some kind of mirth, and was about to investigate when a voice from behind reminded them both of the cause.

"Sorry," said Mr Michaels, having found some courage in the absence of their attention, "who are you two?" His knees, only just straightened, almost buckled beneath him as the two sets of eyes swung to his corner. There was a silent pause as everyone returned to the situation in hand.

"Right!" Alter said, his voice projecting above the uncertainty. "Sorry, I'm the Demon Alter, a Demon of Death," he explained, offering the man his hand and firmly shaking his ineffective grip. "Hi. And this," he motioned to Morana, "is the angel Morana, also of Death." Morana fluttered her fingers at Mr Michaels, who felt none the wiser for the introductions as he mirrored her wave, though Morana had already returned her attentions to Alter.

"So, why are we both here together, at the same time?"

"Simultaneously all at once?" he mocked her, before confessing, "I don't know. Maybe he changed his mind mid final breath?" Both Death workers turned to look hard at the man who was attempting to use the red wallpaper for support and comfort.

"I didn't?" He squeaked with a dry tongue, but neither of them appeared to note his attempted protest.

"Or maybe..." Alter began, not taking his eyes from the man.

"...He's an arguer!" Morana finished, her shoulders slumping with disappointment. "Oh God, no, not an arguer, not today! I'm already running late and I really wanted to get home to watch Animal Hospital tonight."

"I did tell you, you should learn how to set the recorder for these things."

Once again, feeling emboldened by their distraction, Mr Michaels tried to make sense of the situation.

"Hang on, if you're the angel of death, how can you have time to-"

"Oh, no no no!" Alter interrupted him before he could make an obvious mistake. "Not *the* angel, *an* angel. *Bi-hi-hig* difference."

Morana frowned at his hackneyed explanation, but could not disagree with it.

"He's right. We're..." she considered for a moment before deciding on, "sort of localised shift workers really."

Alter nodded seriously, then leaned in towards Mr Michaels to add in a theatrical aside: "You would not want her to be the only angel of death! You'd only be allowed to die after 9 AM and before Animal Hospital." He smiled widely, and Mr Michaels laughed uncomfortably under his intense gaze.

"I'm not that bad," Morana pouted from behind the two men, a little hurt as much by the truth of it.

"Yes, you are," Alter continued, playing oblivious to any distress he might be causing her. Morana's pout grew and she watched her antagonist for any sign of remorse. Realising none was coming, she decided to move on.

"Look," she said, turning to Mr Michaels, who took a small shuffle back into his safety zone, "the thing is, if you are an arguer - and you have every right to be-" she conceded gracefully...

"What's an arguer?" the man interrupted with a stutter.

Alter sighed with bored impatience, sending shivers down the man's spine as he suddenly wished he'd never said a word. The demon explained, without taking a breath, as if reciting from an invisible prompt card before him, the same indifferent tedium to his tone:

"Someone who decides to use his final few moments of connection to this mortal coil to argue against the judgement meted out to him on the grounds that (a) he doesn't agree with it (b) he doesn't believe in God, Our Great Lord Satan, Heaven and/or Hell or (c) he wants reincarnation."

Even as he finished, Alter still didn't appear to take in a breath of relief and the man watched in wonder. Then he remembered how important the words had been in relation to his predicament and began to think them through, creating another uncomfortable pause. Morana watched him with an awkward smile; Alter crossed his arms and tapped his left foot against the deep purple carpet.

"Can I have reincarnation, please?" Mr Michaels finally decided.

"No!" the other two responded in chorus.

"Sorry," Morana broke in apologetically, "I mean, yes, of course, you *can* have that-"

"No he can't!" Alter interjected, almost stamping his impatient foot through the floor.

"Yes, he *can* have that," Morana repeated in a placating voice, "but my point is-"

"Anyway," the dead man once again interrupted her flow, growing a little frustrated by the mixed messages he was receiving, "I thought death was supposed to be all dark tunnels with bright lights and angels singing and family members greeting you at the end..."

"...Cotton wool clouds and endless supplies of chips and ice cream?" Alter prolonged the man's false hopes through gritted teeth. "Well, we are so so sorry to disappoint you-"

"Erm..." Morana spotted her opposition's fingers flexing aggressively, as if waiting for just the right moment to grip the man's neck and squeeze. She stepped between the two males, smiling widely, as if that were enough to relieve the tension. "It is for some people, I suppose," she said, keeping a careful eye on the reactions of both men. "But not everyone. No two deaths are alike, just like no two births are. Apparently."

"Really?" asked Alter, as unaware of this birth theory as his colleague clearly was, since her response was an unconvincingly positive:

"Mmm."

"Well can't *I* have a death like that?" Mr Michaels requested his second choice.

"No!" exclaimed the increasingly irritated Alter.

"But I'm not even sure I want to die yet!" the man wailed.

Alter practically spluttered with disbelief and annoyance at the man's attitude.

"Well tough! Too bloody late! You don't get to choose that! Look!" he pointed unceremoniously at the man's still body, sprawled across the bed, making Mr Michaels wince with horror and discomfort. "You've been dead for... I don't know how long now! All this time we've wasted!" He turned imploringly to Morana, who was feeling just as uncomfortable around the growing conflict. "Honestly, I am so fed up with people today. Only two centuries ago they read up on these things, they were prepared when I arrived. You remember?" Morana nodded, putting on her listening face while wondering just how much worse the day could get. "Now it's all "I don't want to" and "Can't it wait"!" He spun back to Mr Michaels, who was shocked to find his own face only inches away from the demon's. "Well no, actually, no it can't!"

"Look," Morana called out, trying yet again to assuage them, "my point was," she pushed Alter away from Mr Michaels and smiled soothingly at him, "if you *are* going to argue, you really should take a look at both your options anyway. And I would recommend starting with Hell. A lot of people just assume Heaven is the better option - all those white walls and soft furnishings - you know, but it really isn't for everyone." This had never been her point at all and even as she spoke it she could hardly believe the words were hers. Yet it seemed like the only good solution to the problem. Alter was ready for a fight - if not with Mr Michaels, then with her - and this way she might even win a soul. For a change. It had to be the best solution, didn't it?

"And Hell," she continued, not knowing how she could possibly retract now anyway, "with a little imagination-" But before she could finish, she was interrupted by the bleeping of her PDA. She winced at the sound, which was fast becoming her own private torture.

"I tell you what," she said, pulling out the PDA, glancing quickly at the screen, before shoving it back behind her (Mr Michaels wondering exactly where it fitted within her costume, but deciding not to ask), "I've got a ten minute break coming up in, ooh, about an hour. That should give you plenty of time to go along with Alter now." She turned to Alter with a hard look on her face. "Under absolutely *no* obligations," she pronounced in a voice like a headmistress to a naughty schoolboy. Alter's smile and shrug of innocence didn't fool her, but she had no time to reprimand him further. "Have a look around, and I'll come and meet you in an hour. If you still want me to? OK?"

Mr Michaels found himself nodding in agreement, while his insides - or at least his spiritual guts, which still seemed to mimic the churning of his old tissue, muscles and organs - shrank with uncertainty and terror.

"Great!" Morana smiled with relief. "Got to rush." She began to make her way out, stopping before Alter as she left to instruct him once more: "Be nice."

Add Vices (Part 1)

Morana sat at the table, looking as down as she felt. Her wings were no longer visible, though she had yet to change out of her work clothes. A big piece of chocolate cake sat tantalisingly before her, but she could do little more than pick at it with her fork. Even the sound of her housemate striding in did little to lift her head or spirits. Alter was smiling after another successful day of work. He threw his door keys and PDA into a carefully placed ashtray by the kitchen door, opened the fridge, extracted a cold beer from its resting shelf and relaxed with a sigh of contentment into the chair opposite the angel. The can opened with a fizz and Alter took a noisy glug. He let out another satisfied sigh, this time exhaling loudly with that "Ahh" sound drinkers make from their first acceptable sip. Still Morana didn't acknowledge him, which was almost becoming irksome. He studied her for a moment, the half-eaten cake before her being smashed and prodded, the occasional high-pitched squeak as the scrape of the fork missed its target. Eventually, he could take it no longer.

"Good day?" he asked. Morana mumbled a downhearted negative into her plate of food. "Oh well," he responded with minimal sympathy. "Better luck next time." He took another swig of his beer, but as the can lowered to the table he noticed the pout on Morana's lips was genuine. Her cheeks and eyes were tinged red and the horrible fear that she could start to cry at any moment suffocated him until it eased out a modicum of sympathy. "What's happened?"

Morana looked up, checked his face for sarcasm, then returned to her cake.

"I think I'm in a lot of trouble," she sobbed.

"Why?" he asked guiltily.

"I got so behind after this morning's late start, I decided to pick up the pace a bit this afternoon."

"Ah." Alter could sense what was coming.

"Took a few souls a smidgen too early." She looked up again. "You know, before they'd had enough time for-"

"Famous last words?" Alter couldn't help interrupting for the fun of it. Morana nodded helplessly. It was a rookie mistake, one that would be fine if she hadn't been doing this job for as long as she had - or, of course, if she were a demon, but...

"I may have been doing that a lot lately," she confessed.

Alter pulled a face of awkward sympathy. "Well..." He paused, trying to think of the right thing to say. "A few less last words won't kill anyone." Alter grinned, chuckling internally at his own joke, but his face straightened quickly as he caught Morana's disapproving scowl.

"I've been summoned," she sighed dejectedly. "I'm pretty sure that's it for me. They're going to strip me of my wings. I am out of here." She spoke in a morose voice, slow and clipped, that in different circumstances might have sent him to sleep. But he pulled himself out of the gloom she was creating.

"Nah," he dismissed reassuringly, before ruining it with a curious: "Can they?"

Morana ignored his piqued interest in angelic politics, continuing instead with her own glum whining.

"I'm constantly late. I keep ruining people's final moments. I'm winning less and less souls! I'm so bad, I've even got out-of-area demons getting to souls before me. I told you what happened the other day?"

Alter and Morana looked up toward the ceiling as if the memory were playing on the white scrolling artex...

Emma Walker

Interlude: The Devil Came For Georgia

A little girl's body lay under thin pink sheets, surrounded by teddies and condolence cards. From outside the doorway came the sound of sobbing parents. Morana's heart ached with the pain and sadness as she looked down at the youngster, her perfect little hands crossed over her chest and her eyes delicately closed. No matter how many times she dealt with such souls, it never got any easier. Through the doorway, the same little girl appeared, walking in behind Morana, making the angel jump as she skipped into her line of vision. No matter how many times it happened... Morana pulled herself together. She had a job to do.

"Hello," she said, smiling down kindly at the girl, "Phew! You made me jump!" She liked to try and make light with young children, who, somewhat disconcertingly, were often far less nervous than she was. The young girl watched Morana expectantly. "Erm... No need to be afraid. My name is Morana the Angel and I've come to take you to a better place, where-"

"Now Georgia, what have I told you about talking to strangers, hmm?" Morana almost jumped through the roof. The voice had sounded without warning from behind her, an unctuous voice that sent shivering ripples through her feathers. She turned nervously to face the demon who had just wandered in.

"Who the hell are you?" she asked before realising her anxious error. "I mean..." The demon ignored her fumbling, more interested in beckoning over the young girl, who happily complied. Morana watched with astonishment. "Hang on!" she protested. "Georgia, erm, I don't think you want to do that." The young girl accepted the demon's hand just as easily, and Morana nearly choked. "Or that!" she insisted.

"Oh, it's OK," the demon assured her with slimy confidence. "Georgia and I go way back, don't we my dear?" The little girl nodded and stuck her free thumb into her mouth comfortably, though her eyes showed no sign of fear.

"But... She's only a little girl!" Morana stuttered and stammered her protest in bewilderment, thoroughly disturbed at the demon's attitude.

"I know," the demon replied, raising his eyebrows with a wry smile. "But we made a pact two Christmases ago. And you did so love your Tears and Tantrums baby doll, didn't you?" he cooed to the girl who nodded passively. The demon threw back his head wistfully. "Ah, Christmas. Best time of the year." He brought his attention back to Morana with a jerk of remembrance. "Oh, tell Alter I said hi. It's Abalam, by the way." Morana watched with shock as he made to leave with the girl.

"Wait!" she called after him. "You cannot take a little child because of an innocently foolish pact she made for a plastic doll!"

Abalam turned back to look at her, mock sympathy in his eyes.

"Sorry, little angel. The bottom line is she's more comfortable with me. She recognises me." He patted the girl gently on the crown of her head and she leant into his arm. He cocked his head towards Morana as if to say *See?*, while knowing he needed no words.

"But you're a devil!" Morana exclaimed desperately.

"And I look and act like one," he coolly replied. "You can't blame little Georgia here if you guys have lost your image."

Morana frowned with confusion. Yes he had the horns, and the tail swinging just behind him, occasionally patting the child's back in a disturbing manner. But she had the wings, she had the halo and the white glowing outfit. How could she not look like an angel? As if reading her mind, Abalam motioned towards a condolence card with a picture of two chubby cherubs smiling sadly out of it. He shrugged at her despondency and once more made to leave.

"I've got chubby cheeks!" she remonstrated.

"But you forgot your halo," he called back over his shoulder. Morana grabbed at the crown of her head in panic. There, as ever, sat her working halo. She glared angrily at the demon's back, then recalled her real job here was not to be fighting him.

"Look at *me*, Georgia," she begged the departing girl. "I've got chubby cheeks, too. I'm a real angel! See?" She let her wings spread out behind her majestically, but to no avail. Abalam smiled smugly as he and Georgia dissolved through the wall...

Add Vices (Part 2)

Morana and Alter's eyes lowered from the ceiling to meet each other's gaze. Her eyes were filled with sadness at the plight of the poor innocent girl; all her fault. He, meanwhile, was smiling at the excellent work of his colleague - especially the bit where he made Morana think she'd forgotten her halo! Brilliant!

Morana scowled at him and he straightened his face and returned a look of pity.

"I *have* got chubby cheeks," Morana mumbled down at her cake mess.

"I know," Alter patted her arm. "And I've spoken to Abalam, and he has promised he won't do that to you again. And I really do think he means it this time," he falsely consoled her, knowing full well Abalam would never make such a promise. Although he *was* a little unhappy that another demon would take advantage of Morana like that. He felt a certain attachment to the angel, a certain possessiveness toward her torment. Abalam didn't know her the way he did after all. Although, the halo thing...

Morana sobbed loudly.

"Come on, now," Alter continued, taking hold of her hand and squeezing it in his. "I'm sure it won't come to anything. You've been summoned loads of times and it hasn't come to anything. Has it?"

She knew he was trying to cheer her up, but as ever his choice of words left much to be desired. She shook her head glumly.

"Well then," he said, as if all was indeed now well again. Morana looked up and took in his earnest expression.

"Since when do you care what happens to me?"

"What? I do care!" Alter sat back in mock affront. It was true they were on opposite sides of the business, and he often found good cause to wind her up. But he had come to see his role in her existence as more than beneficial. She was, after all, a very naive little thing. "You're my roomy," he said, reaching over to bat her shoulder playfully. "I've just got used to having you here. I *like* having you here." For once, there was no lie in his comment. He really did like having her there, although perhaps not always for the best of reasons.

"Really?" she swallowed down a sob.

"Yeah. I mean..." He paused for a moment to think about the reasons. "You make me laugh. You're a good cook." He took the unemployed fork out of Morana's hand and slid the mushed cake over to his side of the table. "Why don't you let me help you out?"

He scooped up a large chunk of chocolate crumbs and shoved it in his mouth.

"By eating my cake?" she asked, with a hint of aggravation at his impolitely acquiring it.

"If it helps," he smiled, swelling with the mouthful, crumbs decorating his lips and teeth. "For starters," he added, mollifying her before her annoyance could grow. "But I could also let a few souls go your way for a change?"

Morana blinked at him, surprised by this incredibly generous offer. But before she could respond another thought hit her like a gust of wind.

"Shh... Ugar! I forgot to come back for Mr Michaels, didn't I!" She slumped back in her chair. "Oh, I am in so much trouble," she groaned.

"No," Alter calmly dismissed her worries.

"Was he alright?" she asked with concern.

"Erm..." Alter tried to think of the best way to answer. "Yes? I'm sure he's settling in by now." But Morana could hear the pretence.

"Dammit!" she cursed, causing Alter to look up with surprise, since she rarely resorted to such language. And it always made him smile in its irony. He tried very hard to keep his lips from curling up this time.

"Look," he said, returning to his offer, "over the next few weeks I'll let you know where the easiest convertibles are. And I'll conveniently miss a few appointments." He poked the metal fork in her direction with each comment, just to emphasise his sincerity.

"You'd do that for me?" she asked, unable to spot any signs of insincerity in his tone.

"Yeah, why not?" he casually agreed through another mouthful of cake. "I could always take up smoking again, have a few fag breaks when you're in the area, and before you know it your soul tally will be right up there with..." He paused, trying to think of the best example, but could only come up with "a normal angel of death." Luckily Morana missed the veiled insult.

"Aw, thanks."

"No problem," he said, scraping his chair back across the kitchen floor and standing up. "I'm sure you'd do the same for me." Alter winked, then walked off towards the living room with the cake. "So what shall we watch tonight?" he called back through the wall. "Psycho, American Werewolf in London, or American Psycho?" Horror films were, in Alter's opinion, part of her earthly education. She still reacted so badly to death and it simply wasn't good enough in her job. Plus, he knew how much she hated them, yet was too polite to refuse him.

Today, however, Morana didn't mind at all. She grinned happily, touched by her housemate's offer, almost allowing herself to believe it was the answer to all her current woes. She stood up and made her way over to the fridge.

"You choose," she called back happily to Alter, pulling out a much bigger slice of 'Good For You: Death By Chocolate' cake and returning to the table with a beaming smile across her face.

The Stars In The Night Sky

Later that evening, somewhere above the neighbourhood rooftops, Morana met for a talk with the angel Franklin, renowned throughout the Heavens for his guidance and support of unfortunate cherubs. As they conversed, the clouds cleared to reveal a sky glowing with bright stars, twinkling with every word they spoke...

"You sent for me, sir?" came the voice of Morana.

"Yes, Morana," Franklin's voice responded. "Things aren't going too well at the moment, are they?"

"Erm... No?"

"We know you're trying your hardest, Morana. You have a good heart. Which is why we cannot refuse you yet another chance. But this time must be different. You have two weeks in which to do better. Your spirit is pure, but your will is too easily deceived. We've been worried for some time about the influence of that demonic housemate of yours."

"Oh, he's OK, really. He's quite decent underneath."

The sound of Franklin's heavy, disappointed sigh radiated across the sky.

"What's that book you're holding?"

"The Da Vinci Code. Alter lent it to me. He says it's about-"

Franklin flashed impatiently, almost turning supernova red.

"Morana! Just do a good job over the next two weeks, and we'll overlook these complaints."

"Oh, thank you, sir. Thank you."

A Boeing 747 flew southbound across the path of stars, rivalling their twinkling with its flashing lights and drowning out Morana's gratitude with its engines; thus the conversation was officially deemed to have ended.

Caution

"Hey! You're back," Alter greeted his housemate as she returned to ground level, shuffling into the living room. He was sat on their sofa, already part of the way through American Werewolf in London, having decided not to wait for Morana, just in case.

She nodded by way of reply and remembering the severity of her meeting, he paused the film and turned to give her his full attention.

"How did it go?"

Morana slumped on to the sofa beside him.

"I got cautioned," she glowered. Alter pursed his lips sympathetically.

"But you haven't lost your wings?"

"No."

"Well, there you go then!" he said in his usual, dismissive tone. "I told you it would be fine." Satisfied with this outcome, he returned to the TV, unpausing the film. Angel sighed heavily as he watched the mauling. She picked at the edge of the sofa, a dull scraping sound emanating beneath her nails. Alter tried very hard to concentrate, but the sound of her material scratching and the feel of her melancholy against his left side made it virtually impossible.

"I'm being appraised for the next two weeks," she mumbled over the sound of palpitating music and screams. "If I don't do well..."

Alter paused the film again. More effort was needed to placate the female.

"Oh, you can easily do well in two weeks. And my offer still stands. Easy pickings?" Morana remembered Franklin's warnings regarding her housemate. She knew she shouldn't really trust him as much as she did. But what other option was there to guarantee her job?

"Really?" she asked.

"Yeah. 'Course. As long as you promise not to tell anyone?" For the first time, Morana realised just how much he was offering her. Granted, she would be in trouble with her superiors if they were caught out, yet she'd forgotten he would be too - and probably much worse.

"Well. I promise *I* won't tell anyone. Although, I can't help Anyone-" she pointed upwards, "noticing."

"Oh. Yeah." Alter grimaced at the ceiling. He returned his eyes to the TV with a shudder. "I meant anyone on my side."

"Oh, well, I definitely won't be telling anyone on *your* side. I don't even like talking to anyone on your side. Obviously apart from you," she added, rubbing his arm reassuringly, inducing an unwanted scowl from Alter, which she, as usual, didn't take personally. He nodded appreciatively when her hand finally left his arm. Morana paused suspiciously as he returned to watching his film. She examined him cautiously, Franklin's words mingling with her need to succeed.

"I don't mean to sound..." she scrambled through her vocabulary, "ungrateful or... unnecessarily suspicious, but what am I going to have to do in return?"

Alter chuckled to himself, then frowned very hard.

"Actually, I hadn't thought that far ahead. But whatever it is, I'm sure it'll be good. What have you got to lose?"

"My soul?"

"Not for the next two weeks," Alter quipped mischievously, sending chills through Morana's stomach.

Death By Chocolate

Bring Out Your Dead

Early the next morning, a lone fly buzzed and bounced about the window pane, curious as to the nature of its entrapment, the sun rise glistening against its wings and warming its tapping legs. It stopped on a used plate, reaching out with its tongue, momentarily impressed by this new discovery. The tranquillity of this insect's morning was suddenly shattered by the distinct sound of a foghorn from the next room, followed by the unnecessary howling of the sounds initiator, a large male creature, throwing arms and legs in the air as he bounded away from his crime. The demon looked down at the plate, the startled fly... And that's the last thing the insect remembered of the whole incident.

Having disposed of a pesky fly from yesterday's unwashed crockery, wondering why Morana would have left the job unfinished, Alter moved to the freezer, took out a ready-meal full English breakfast, and placed it appreciatively into the microwave. While he watched the machine spin and zap, Morana joined the demon, shuffling in, half-asleep, bleary eyed, a dash of blood by her nose and a tissue in her hand. Alter stood to attention as she entered. He clapped his hands together with an excited readiness.

"So, the plan is, I let you have first dibs on all the easy souls – provided you get there on time." He noted Morana's dishevelled appearance, the red smudge between her nostrils and lips, and shuddered. This was going to be so much harder than he wanted it to be. "You're going to have to get yourself up early in the mornings, 'cause I really can't deal with your random nosebleeds." He shuddered again. No matter how many times it happened, it just seemed wrong for an angel to bleed like that.

Morana wiped her nose sleepily (little did Alter know she used the bleeding to her advantage more often than not). It was still far too early. "Deal," she agreed. "And while we're on the subject, can I put in a request for no bloody bodies please?"

"So just standard natural causes and died-in-their-sleep types then?"

"Yes please."

Alter crossed his fingers behind his back. "Deal," he agreed as the microwave completed its toil with a ding.

⌛

Alter was as good as his word. At least in terms of helping her out with the acquisition of souls. That evening, he stood casually outside a terraced house, smoking a cigarette, intermittently glowing in the blue flashing lights of an ambulance and two police cars. From somewhere in the house behind him, the distinct sound of Morana's scream could be heard, followed by a muffled and nervous "Er, no need to be afraid?". Alter could not help but giggle for the umpteenth time that day. As a set of police constables made their way tentatively up the stairs, the angel emerged through the front door. She leant against the doorpost, clutching her stomach, but soon caught sight of the grinning demon. He took a last drag of his cigarette and dropped the dying embers on to the garden grass as he made his way over to Morana.

"You *bars*-"

"Careful" he warned her before she could yet again break her vow of non-cursing. "Did you get him?" he motioned up towards the bathroom window, which was now the scene of multiple silhouettes against the yellow-glowing blind.

"Yes," Morana answered through gritted teeth. Just behind her, a man stumbled out through his own front door for the last time, slightly shaken, but looking happy enough. He was momentarily taken aback by the presence of Alter, who cocked his head with a smile of greeting, before turning back to Morana.

"Thank you?" he prompted her sarcastically, and received a scowl in return as she lead the recently departed away. No sooner had they commenced their journey than a stretcher appeared through the door, flanked by two ambulance men, three knives protruding through the plaid suit of the body riding upon it.

"It's the last time, I promise!" Alter called after her as she dissolved with her latest soul.

⧖

The following day was much the same. Alter skulked at doorways, peeking through expectantly. Morana's scream and jittery introduction could be heard as Alter laughed roguishly to himself.

That evening, Morana sat at the kitchen table, dozing peacefully. A plate of chocolate crumbs rested on the table before her. Alter entered, smiling and cocky as ever, threw his PDA, keys and an empty cigarette packet into the ashtray. The noise startled Morana out of her light dreams.

"Good day?" he asked, knowing the answer full well.

"What? Oh," Morana rubbed her eyes. "Yeah," she answered unconvincingly, yawning widely. "This has been the longest week of my existence."

"Only one more week to go," he reassured her and she shuddered at the thought of another week like that one. Which, considering she was under the instruction of a demon, was very likely.

"I never realised there could be so many murders in such a short space of time," she moaned.

"Oh yes," Alter confirmed jovially. "Statistically, there are around ninety-five deliberate murders in the world every day, you know."

"Really?" Morana asked, horrified.

Alter smiled to himself. "It's a rough estimate. Based on an average good day. Hey, don't worry," he added, noting her look of dismay, "I said I'd get you the easy ones, didn't I? And murders are definitely easier. They expect to see an angel. So they can register their complaint about the injustice of it all."

"So I've found out," she agreed unhappily.

"Anyway. I can't help you tomorrow," he suddenly declared, causing her to feel just as much discomfort as the possibility of another day with his help. "Been warned," he explained. "Bit of a big fish to catch apparently. Could mean promotion, so not one I can share. But you should be meeting your targets by now, right?"

Before she had the chance to contend this, Morana was distracted by a bleep from her PDA. She'd virtually forgotten its existence recently, so busy had she been with Alter's pickings.

"Mmm," she said in the general direction of Alter, while her eyes perused the screen. "That's OK. I might sleep in tomorrow." But Alter had already left her to her musings. Two bright red words flashed up at her: "URGENT SUMMONS".

The Court Of Angels

To the untrained eye at first glance, the Court of Angels was not too dissimilar to a grand cathedral. Morana stood at one end of the long nave, rows seemingly stretching on for miles to each side of her. There, sat in those countless pews, were all fellow angels (who could spare the time). In the rear pews sat the younger, fresh-faced cherubs, followed in the central seats by the more experienced angels, and finally, huddled into the very front rows were the archangels and those ancients who could remember the first aeons of existence, long before time began.

Some way in the distance was the altar, with the resemblance of a courtroom judge's bench. The space around the courtroom was white and vaporous, as though clouds were constantly drifting by to observe the proceedings before nonchalantly passing on. Not the clouds of the known type that hang lazily about the sky, but clouds that brought to mind a gigantic bowl of whipped double cream. Cream which looks strong enough to walk upon, but, should you try to, you would slowly sink beneath its fluffy, light coolness, and all you would want to do is stick out your tongue and lick...

Above, like a sudden crack in these same clouds, a pure blue sky-ceiling looked down upon them, contrasting so sharply with the darkness of the world she had just left, it confused Morana's sense of time. She took a deep breath and cautiously began to walk down the central isle, saying hello to every angel she recognised as she passed them. In turn, they smiled back, but with an air of pity that she innocently refused to notice or acknowledge. Reaching the very end of the pews, she halted. The judge's bench towered above her, still some distance ahead. At the sound of a bell of perfect size and tone, an Archangel appeared from behind the bench, took his seat, and everyone else in the room, with the sole exception of Morana, took this as a signal to sit as well.

The Archangel was a mature man with the air of a kindly but despairing schoolteacher about him. He would really prefer not to have to reprimand his charges, would prefer indeed to gain their respect rather than their fear; yet, nevertheless, he was well aware of their inadequacies and his need to fix them. Under his all-knowing gaze, Morana instantly felt like such a pupil. She gripped her hands in front of her, hunched her shoulders and shuffled her feet uncomfortably against the smooth floor.

The Archangel cleared his throat and looked down at Morana, his silver hair flowing about his long face.

"Angel Morana, do you know why you have been summoned here?" His voice was a strange mixture of calm quiet and projected clarity, which Morana, like many other angels present in the Court, could not help but admire. He waited patiently for her answer.

"Erm... No?"

He took a deep breath, sat back in his chair and slowly opened a buff-coloured file before him.

"We've had a serious complaint against you," he explained, reading from the paperwork, "from one Mr Michaels." He looked down at Morana. "The complaint has been upheld, I'm afraid. Can't be avoided. He says that you promised to collect him after he had spent an hour with the Demon Alter in Hell, at which point you were to bring him to Heaven." The Archangel rubbed his eyes wearily, not knowing where to start with the problems that entailed. "You never returned to him. Is this true?"

There was, of course, no way out of it. "Yes," she answered despondently. A ripple of noise echoed from behind her, making her cheeks glow red with shame.

"Aside from the obvious horror such a-" the Archangel grappled for the right words a moment, "an *agreement* suggests, why did you not return for him?"

"I only remembered quite a few hours afterwards," she confessed, feeling her feet wobble, as if on the aforementioned clouds of cream, incapable of doing anything right to stop herself from sinking and sticking out a helpless tongue...

"Then why didn't you collect him when you had remembered?" the Archangel barked through her reverie.

"Because," Morana began, trying to picture the event clearly in her mind. Why hadn't she? "Because I spoke to the Demon Alter and he assured me that everything had been sorted?" Another wave of muttering arose from the pews.

"And you believed him?" the Archangel asked in amazement.

"Yes," she replied.

"Why?"

Morana shrugged. "Why should he lie?"

"Because he's a demon!" The Archangel's voice rose louder than ever. "They all lie! They also cheat, deceive, destroy-" he paused in his desperate outburst, remembering the case in hand. "It is our job to make sure they cannot do those things, not give them every opportunity to! Concerns about your spending time with this particular demon have been raised before. We had hoped that it would not come to this, but-" He was distracted in his outburst of morals by Morana's hand waving in the air, beckoning for a moment to respond. "Yes?"

"I just wanted to say," she began meekly, "I don't think that's fair. Granted, yes, he has a bad side. He's misguided and a little... difficult at times. But he's not *all* bad." A deathly silence followed, eventually broken by the distant sound of an uncomfortable cough from one of the elder archangels. The Presiding Archangel looked down his nose at the accused and sighed.

"I commend your ability to forgive, Angel Morana, but he *is* a demon. It is in his *nature* to be nothing but bad."

"I disagree," she argued, and a collective intake of breath resounded behind her. Mumbles of shock and surprise gradually fluttered between the many onlookers. "In fact," Morana had to raise her voice a little over the new din, "over the past week he's been helping me out with-"

"Helping you out?" The archangel repeated, causing the noise of the room to increase yet further. He banged his gavel and eyed the audience sharply until they all fell silent again. Morana needed no instruction to do the same - she already recognised she'd said too much and was hoping a hole might appear in the perfect floor to suck her quickly back down to earth. High above her, the presiding Archangel was in whispered conference with another ancient.

"Oh yes," he said pointedly. "We know about your little deal over this week. Not strictly appropriate - especially since you are on a two week probation because of him!"

"But that's my point! He didn't have to help me, but he did." It was too late to back down now, she realised. "Angels and demons were once one and the same. There was no distinction! We all know that, though we choose to forget it. Surely, if *we* are capable of good things, then so are they?"

The courtroom spectators were instantly stirred to debate this fact, the ancient archangels huffing and guffawing with displeasure, while some of the younger sort questioned the merit of her words. For a moment, Morana felt like a revolutionary. Perhaps, after this meeting, a whole new aeon would emerge in which angels and demons would stop the fight between good and evil and allow a peace to rein? Surely it could happen…? She wondered if any of the older angels had ever witnessed such an impertinent young radical in the Court before… And then she remembered. There was that one time, *right before the Fall*… She looked around the pews and a tight panic gripped her insides. The last thing she wanted was to be held responsible for the next major crisis!

"I just worry that we angels may have all become a little cynical over the centuries," she announced over the noise to those who were still willing to listen. The presiding archangel, who had watched the proceedings below him with a mixture of despair and amusement, called back his authority with a bellow for silence that had instant affect.

"This is not a debate about the personality traits of demons. We have enough trouble keeping up with the human characters!" There was a ripple of polite laughter before the archangel returned to the paperwork before him. "A serious complaint has been raised against you, Morana. Now, I am aware that you are currently on the aforementioned probation period. It is my ruling, therefore, that after those two weeks have ended we consider moving you from Death duties to something more... appropriate to your nature."

Morana looked up at him, crestfallen, but accepting his judgement as was befitting an angel of her status.

"You have one week left," he confirmed. "This is your last chance to show us that you can do better. Then you will report back here. Understood?" She nodded silently. "Use your week wisely," he guided. "And if you want to do that-" his face grimaced at the very thought, "that *demon friend* of yours any good, convert him. Convert him or destroy him. Vanquish him for the good of mankind. Those are and always have been your affirmed duties. Consider the following week a test. Understood?"

Emma Walker

Confessions Of A Loser

Alter returned home late that night, a contented smile on his lips. He'd spent a more than pleasant evening painting the town red with some demon colleagues he hadn't seen for a while, enticing all sorts of foolish young innocents into binge drinking contests, strip clubs, and beds that were not their own. He was headed toward the kitchen for a well-earned midnight snack, but found himself stopping short at the living room door. Morana was inside, dimly lit by a single table lamp, dropping items randomly into a cardboard box. He watched her efforts for a moment, trying to decide between food and curiosity. The latter, predictably, got the better of him. He tapped the doorframe gently.

"Hey! Still up?" he called in rhetorically. Then, nodding towards the slowly filling cardboard box, asked: "What's going on?"

"It's over," she said sullenly.

"What is?"

She didn't answer, her focus instead remaining on the box.

Death By Chocolate

"All the books on death and dying are yours and all the poetry books are mine, right?"

"What?" he snapped, mildly impatient now that he'd given up on a snack for this. "What are you going on about?"

"I was summoned," she finally explained. "They know about the deal."

"What deal?" He asked, then promptly remembered. "Our deal?" He thought about this for a moment, a slight fear making his coccyx twitch. What if his lot knew about the deal too? No one had said anything that evening. He was tempted to release his tail, an air of defiance trying to mask his nerves. "So? What about all the souls you've saved?"

"Doesn't count. You gave them to me. They have to come of their own accord."

"Rubbish!" He dismissed. There was no way, after all the effort and unnecessary generosity he'd put in, that he was going to let them disregard it all. He walked across the room and gave his housemate a hug. "Look, it will work out, I'm sure."

"I have one more week left here," she explained. "That's it."

"We'll think of something," he reassured her. "I'll stay out of your way tomorrow so you can bag a few *willing* ones." He looked down at the contents of the box. "Confessions of a Sinner is mine."

"I'm sleeping in tomorrow," she said, staring at the claimed book.

"Good for you," he said, giving her one more squeeze before finally disappearing into the kitchen for his delayed snack. Morana slowly reached into the box, extracted the book and returned it to the shelf.

Death By Chocolate

Sinner Man

The following morning, Morana slept, unusually without disturbance, in her nice warm bed beneath a fluffy white quilt that billowed gently over her limbs and torso. There was no sign of blood to her nose and no foghorn in Alter's hand as he crept quietly past her bedroom and skipped to the front door. His palm was instead occupied with his PDA, reminding him of today's important client - the big one; the soul of the season.

Only moments after his departure, Morana was awoken by the piercing bleeps of her own PDA. She rolled onto her back, yawned widely and stretched her fingers up towards the ceiling, her right hand continuing the arc downwards until it came into contact with the source of the noise on her bedside table. She tapped at it randomly until it went quiet, then allowed her fingers to grip its edges and carry it vertically aloft. She opened her eyes for the first time and looked up at the screen, which slowly came into focus as her tired pupils adjusted. The display was upside down. Morana, feeling confused and slightly annoyed at being woken so early from her planned lie in, turned the machine the right way up and clicked to open the latest communication. She blinked heavily as she scanned the message.

"France...?"

⌛

Meanwhile, her demon housemate was stood upon a cliff edge, its white chalk face plummeting below him. A fresh sea breeze massaged his face and contours, somehow unaffecting his deep red tail and taut wings, with their dark, almost black veins snaking through them. He lowered his PDA into the pocket of his sharp-looking suit.

"Brittany," he confirmed. He took a deep, pleasurable breath before leaping out over the waves...

⌛

Back in her cosy bedroom, Morana had managed to rouse herself, and was sat on the edge of her bed, still yawning indelicately. The PDA rested on the pillow beside her, the same pillow that had once supported her tired head. She looked down at the screen, still blinking with confusion.

"Why on earth would I be sent to France?" she asked the empty room, which chose not to reply. She slowly rose, standing awkwardly, stumbling toward the bedroom door with the full intention of beginning her workday. Yet somehow her legs bypassed the exit, preferring instead to carry her to the other side of the bed, where she instinctively pulled back the cover and crawled beneath it, nestling her head down beside the PDA. Just as her eyes closed with a satisfying sigh, the PDA beeped and flashed impatiently in her face.

"Oh, all right!" she groaned.

A short while later, following one chocolate-toffee finest yoghurt, a small mocha and a quick wash and change - consistently interrupted by the increasingly painful, high-pitched squeaks and squeals of the PDA - Morana found herself standing before a large converted chapel in Brittany, a lonely looking figure, surrounded by fields and orchards, the nearest houses just visible at the end of a narrow roadway in the distance. The sky was hidden with a blanket of flat, off-white cloud. Now and then, thin shards of sunlight seeped through, momentarily piercing the ground before swiftly being snuffed out again.

⌛

Whilst she was taking in the outdoor scenery, Alter was looking down from the balcony of a split-level room, admiring the rich, impressive interior of his newest client's house. He turned back on himself and sauntered into the bedroom.

⌛

Morana stepped through the heavy wooden front door - a far more security-conscious replica of the original church door, she suspected. A short corridor led her into an open-planned living and dining room, flanked to one side by a beautiful fireplace, and to the other by a spiral staircase, leading up to an almost theatrical indoor balcony. She listened for any sounds of mourners or confused souls, but heard nothing. Cautiously, she traversed the room to her left and admired the carefully arranged clutter on the mantelpiece. She picked up, with some surprise, a genuine Oscar statuette.

"Cinema!" she quietly exclaimed, turning the trophy about in her palms, before replacing it gently where she'd found it, looking nervously behind her for a potential audience...

⌛

Alter spread himself out on the plush bed, rubbing his fingers over the silken sheets with a grin of satisfaction.

"Television!" he exclaimed, admiring the huge flat-screen TV on the opposite wall. Whoever this soul was, he had certainly made a fan of Alter with his style of living...

⌛

Walking through the small annex of a kitchen, Morana trailed her finger along the opened pages of a fancy French cookery book.

"Haute Cuisine," she admired, noting the lavish utensils, sparkling clean in their display holders...

⌛

Still in the bedroom, Alter shuffled through some papers on a cherry wood study desk, parting a small pile to reveal a plate from which some mouldy slices of bread and the remnants of their once edible filling stared up uncomfortably.

"A sandwich. Eugh!" He re-hid the leftovers with mild disgust...

⌛

Morana returned to the central open space, admiring the collection of paintings, sketches and photographs that decorated the walls.

"Art," she nodded appreciatively...

⌛

Alter peered through the eyepiece of an expensive white telescope, searching the scene outside through a patch of clear window. The view was dull and he stood up, spinning the equipment carelessly around on its tripod.

"Science," he scoffed...

⌛

On a small, darkened windowsill, Morana found a collection of photographs of various smiling people, but with one repeated face among them all, whom she correctly identified as the owner of the house. At the back of the display was one larger shot of the middle-aged actor in a carefully posed black and white portrait. He was unmistakably good-looking, and even Morana could not prevent a brief moment's covetousness.

"Beauty," she whispered, impressed...

⌛

Perusing the bookshelves above the study desk, Alter was also impressed by the collection of large, leather-bound books resting upon them.

"Brains," he acknowledged, sliding a random book from its place and disturbing a blizzard-fall of dust in the process.

"Maybe not..."

⌛

Tiptoeing up the staircase, Morana caught sight, through the bedroom door, of the beautiful, large stained-glass window, which adorned the rear of the bedroom. There upon it was the impression of Christ, dressed in a loincloth and crown of thorns, hanging heavily from the crucifix, while Mary Magdalene wept at his feet.

"Passion," she thought aloud, moved by the imagery, stepping closer to admire the colouring, so taken in by it that she neglected to see the other occupant of the room sidling in beside her. She felt her feathers ripple slightly and turned slowly to face Alter. His tail lifted instinctively behind him. They looked into each other's familiar faces, the coloured light through the windowpanes marking their flesh, and held a moment's stillness before the image of ultimate sacrifice.

"What the hell are you doing here?" Morana eventually woke from the silence and rounded on him.

"I could ask you the same thing," Alter replied, trying not to show just how surprised he truly was. The accusations pulled them out of the strange spell that had rooted them to the spot. They self-consciously stepped apart and simultaneously pulled out their PDAs. Having checked his own, Alter showed Morana, who compared the identical appointment details with hers.

"Oh no, not this again!" She groaned.

"Well, I was here first," Alter declared, "so why don't I just carry on with the job and you can head home and enjoy the rest of your morning off?"

"It won't matter who got here first if he's an arguer," she reminded him.

"He's not going to be an arguer," Alter disputed, but Morana was already unconvinced. She put her PDA away and began to slump down the stairs.

"Coffee?" she called back behind her.

"Er... Tea?" he requested.

Morana disappeared into the kitchen below, followed by a variety of standard drink-making sounds; the clinking of cups, swishing of water, huffing and bubbling of the kettle. Bored of listening, Alter returned to his curious investigation of the dead man's belongings.

If he *was* to be an arguer, it would do the demon no harm to start building a suitable case for the soul.

"Sugar?" Morana called up the stairs.

"Now what have you done?" Alter yelled back.

"No," explained Morana, making him jump guiltily as she poked her head around the bedroom door. "I mean, do you want sugar?"

"Oh, erm… yes? Three please." They glared at each other suspiciously for a moment, Alter convinced she'd returned to check up on him, while she wondered why he was behaving so strangely. He felt, since they'd lived together almost five months now, she should know how many sugars he took (although with a clearer head he would remember that her ability to retain anything, let alone such little trivia, was always poor); she felt that it would be so much nicer if he would occasionally make *her* a cup of tea. Then she reminded herself how much better it was to give than to receive, smiled at Alter, and disappeared back down the stairs.

Alter sat down on the edge of the bed, once more running his hands over those smooth sheets. He slowly leant forward, letting his head drop between his knees and hitching the blankets up to spy under the bed boards.

"Aha!" He exclaimed happily.

"What?" came Morana's voice from just above him, startling him back up into his seat, his hands now full of magazines. He blinked awkwardly from her to his find a couple of times, then smiled broadly.

"You can go home. He's one of ours," Alter answered, dropping his find beside him on the bed, and taking one of the two cups of hot liquid held by Morana.

"Why?" she asked looking down at the spread. Alter picked up and held out one of the more colourful offending articles for her unmistakable viewing.

"Pornographic magazines," he drawled.

"Oh," said Morana, totally unimpressed. "That doesn't count."

"Eh?"

"New legislation," she explained to his shocked face. "We've had to relax on some rules to keep up with the times. Otherwise we'd never get anyone," she joked lightly.

"So you allow for porn?"

"I know, I know," she agreed with his disbelief. "Don't get me started! They seem to be changing the rules every week these days!"

Alter dropped the magazine despondently back onto the pile. He took a large swig of his tea, and offered a grateful smile to Morana, who joined him in a moment's silent drinking.

And then it occurred to her.

"Something's wrong," she announced dramatically, lowering her cup.

Alter sniffed his tea and shrugged. "Bit milky?"

"No, I mean here. Something's wrong in this house. We've both, for some unknown reason, been sent to meet the same soul... Yet there's no soul lingering here!"

Alter had been so busy forming his claim to the dead man's soul, he'd completely overlooked its absence.

"He's... probably just run off somewhere," he reasoned doubtfully. "Some last-minute regret or something..." Morana watched him grappling for an explanation, like a teacher waiting on a pupil, knowing full well he would fail while still allowing him the chance to try. "Visiting family? Or hiding?"

"No," she shook her head as he came to the end of his hopeful list, wriggling uncomfortably under her patient gaze. "That's not it. His soul's not here at all. But it would have to return to the vicinity of the body soon enough."

"Exactly!" Alter agreed, finally feeling like he'd found an answer.

"So... Where is he?"

Alter's enthusiasm plummeted again. Still, undeterred by the setback, he decided to make the best of it.

"I tell you what, why don't you finish the rest of your day's appointments and I'll wait here for when he comes back?"

"No way!"

"What?" Alter exclaimed with feigned innocence.

"Why don't *you* go, and *I'll* wait here?" she retaliated.

"*Oh-ho* no!"

"Why not?" She asked, pretending to be a little hurt. "You know you can trust me to do the right thing. Besides, I don't have any other appointments. This is it. See?" She showed him her PDA, which confirmed what she had just said. Alter rubbed his chin thoughtfully.

"How about you take all my other appointments then?" Adding, as if he needed to sweeten the deal: "For the rest of the week!" He knew this soul, missing or otherwise, was a big deal and he wasn't prepared to lose his job for one angel. He did, however, know how to make a bargain, and what Morana needed were more souls. He felt certain he was the one to give them to her. He fished out his own PDA, ready to make the perfect trade-off, then frowned as he stared at the screen.

"Hang on," he scratched his head with confusion. "This is *it*."

"This is what?" She asked, only half interested, already having made the decision to refuse.

"This is the only appointment I have today." He scrolled down. "And tomorrow." He scrolled down further. "And the day after..."

Morana was now interested; interested because she had been checking her own PDA while he spoke. They stood and compared. Neither of them could explain it. Both PDAs showed the same thing.

"Damn technology!" Alter cursed, assuming the obvious.

"But that's not possible," Morana blinked, bewildered. "I knew there was something wrong! He's not here!"

"I know." Alter was determined not to become paranoid, despite his fears. "You said."

"No. Not just that. His soul would have to return to the site of the body, right?" She repeated her earlier point.

"Exactly," he repeated in turn, though with far less enthusiasm the second time round.

"So where is it? Where exactly is the body?" She looked hard at him before joining him in a quick visual search around their surroundings, neither of them daring to actually move from where they stood. They already knew the truth of it.

"Right," Alter announced with a desperate urgency, "you look around here; I'll search downstairs."

"Right," she echoed, matching his fearful determination.

They stood for a moment, drinking, finishing off their tea, slamming their cups down simultaneously, and then split up.

And so began the search. In their unspoken panic, they left nothing unturned; the mattress, the mirrors, the sofa cushions, rugs, coffee cups... There was a ridiculous frenzy to their hunt. But two minutes later they found themselves face to worried face, no body having been found.

"I don't understand!" Morana wailed.

"OK," Alter decided, in a deceptively controlled voice, "we need to investigate. We need to work out his last moves, try to ascertain where he might have gone."

Morana nodded in agreement. "How do we do that?"

This was exactly what he had hoped *she* would know how to do, but he was determined not to falter now.

"Get me a photo and a felt-tip pen."

"Right," she concurred, running off to complete his orders.

Emma Walker

The Investigation

Alter stood with his back to Morana, staring out of the window, his hands clasped thoughtfully behind him. Morana sat expectantly on the sofa. Alter spun round, revealing the same posed photo of the house owner she had previously admired, now stuck to the window, complete with a newly scribbled moustache, beard and horns. The actor's name was written in heavy black capitals on the white strip beneath the portrait: "Wilfred Bailey Jr". Morana rolled her eyes at the childish graffiti and Alter's matching childish grin, which quickly dissolved to a serious expression.

"So. What have we got?" he asked her officiously.

Morana looked down at the evidence spread across the coffee table, relaying the sight out loud: "One nearly eaten sandwich. Old." She held up the sandwich on its plate, covered by a plastic forensic bag.

That was all. Alter rubbed his chin thoughtfully.

"And what does that tell us?"

"He doesn't like crusts?" She suggested. Alter turned back to the picture on the window and wrote next to it in clear bold lettering: "NO CRUSTS".

"No Crusts. Good. Now-"

"Oh," she interrupted him, "and I found these biscuits." She held out a plate and he looked down at it disparagingly.

"How are they relevant?" he demanded.

"They're Duchy Originals," she clarified. "Chocolate butterscotch?" she offered again.

"Ooh, yeah," he acknowledged greedily, taking one and stuffing it all into his mouth. "Thank you very much," he said through the chewing, and she accepted his approval by eating one herself. "You know," he added as soon as he'd swallowed, "one thing I will say for you, you were always right about chocolate."

"I know," she chomped. "You should have made it the number one sin."

"Absolutely," he agreed, and they both laughed before simultaneously snapping back to serious mode. "Where were we? Oh yes. Now. What do we need to know about Wilfred Bailey Jr?"

"Where he is?" Morana offered unhelpfully.

Alter ignored Morana's useless point. "There must be some way we can get inside the man's mind..." They thought for a moment, and a knowing smile soon appeared on the demon's lips. "...And I think I know how."

Alter disappeared for a moment, leaving Morana to wonder, but returned very swiftly with a large stack of paper. He placed it down heavily on the coffee table next to the mouldy sandwich. The title sheet sat proudly on the top, showing the descriptive words: "It's My Wonderful Life: An Autobiography. By Wilfred Bailey Jr. DRAFT 1."

"Fresh off the press," Alter motioned to his find proudly. "Found it in the bedroom earlier. All we need to do is check the last page." He was so pleased with his plan that it almost broke Morana's heart to have to bring him back down to earth. Still, she had no choice.

"And how is that reliable?" she asked, listening for the thump of his feet as they slammed into the carpet.

"What do you mean?"

"For one thing," she explained, "we don't know how long ago he finished it. Or if *he* even wrote it. Plus it's an autobiography. Isn't it natural for people to stretch the truth a little in their own story?"

"What are you saying? That he may have ended with "I'm off to the Savoy" when in actual fact he was just popping down to the local chippy?"

Morana arched her eyebrows. "No," she sighed. "I doubt that's the sort of thing he'd end with anyway. But you *have* just given me an idea."

"What?" he asked, happy to be important again.

"There is another place we can look. Somewhere more reliable. But I'll need a computer and the internet." Morana searched the room with her eyes for any sign of a workstation.

"Excellent! Yes," Alter agreed, not wholly sure of her plan. "We can see what he's been looking at on the web, whether he's booked any holidays lately, that sort of thing?"

"Better than that," she smiled, spying exactly what she was looking for. She walked across to a small desk and flipped open an almost invisibly thin laptop, turned it on and started to walk back to the sofa with it.

"Where are you going with that?" Alter asked in a warning tone.

Morana indicated towards the sofa with the corner of the machine. "It's alright," she reassured him, "it's wireless."

Alter shook his head judiciously. "You're already two metres away from the wireless hub," he pointed out. Morana accepted his criticism of the technology, returning the laptop to the desk and sitting down before it. She loaded up the internet as Alter joined her.

"So what are we looking for?" he asked intrigued.

"The Akashik Records," she replied with an air of knowing mystery. "The complete story of every human life as it happens. Online."

"You have access to that?" he asked her, clearly impressed.

"Of course," she said proudly, choosing not to expound any further, despite Alter's sudden respect for her. She typed in the address: "www.akashik.god.org."

"Of course," repeated Alter, this time less impressed at the lack of originality. An aged-looking parchment background appeared on the screen with two far more modern looking boxes in the centre, requesting a username and password.

"Would you turn around please?" Morana did not so much ask as instruct Alter.

"Why?" he asked childishly, for he knew full well.

"I'm not allowed to let you see," she sighed. "I'm in enough trouble because of you as it is."

"Fine," he agreed sulkily, half turning his back on her.

"Properly, please?"

Alter stuck his fingers in his eyes and turned a little further around.

"I don't see why I'm not allowed access anyway," he grunted.

"Yes, you do," she maintained, beginning to type.

"It's not as if I can do anything with it," he continued petulantly.

"Here we go," she announced, entirely ignoring his fruitless moans. "Wilfred Bailey Junior."

"Let's see," he said, spinning back round to face the display before she could say no. But all he saw before him was a screen full of very strange looking, totally unintelligible squiggles and swirls. "What kind of nonsense writing is that?" he complained.

"First Angelics, of course," she rolled her eyes. "Didn't you study classical languages?"

"Ugh," he dismissed. "All those wide vowel sounds. No thanks."

Angel scrolled to the end of the screen, running her fingers against it and over the words, which changed to a readable language in her eyes as she did so. Alter shuffled frustratingly behind her, unable to see.

"So? Where is he?" he demanded.

"Hang on," she rebuffed him patiently, slowly reaching the end of the record. "Ah. I forgot." He stared down enquiringly at her sheepish expression. "I don't know."

"Why not?" he huffed.

"Erm... I don't have real-time access."

"Meaning?"

"Meaning," she explained, "I only know where he was and what he was doing," she paused, lowering her head away from his piercing gaze, "up to twelve hours ago."

Alter shook his head with severe displeasure. So close, and yet delayed to nowhere near. A thought crossed his mind. "But I thought all Akashik records were kept up to the minute? Up to the second even?" He was beginning to wonder if she was lying to him. Perhaps she had worked out where to find Bailey, but wasn't prepared to share? Although she *was* an angel, and therefore prone to telling the truth, he reasoned. Nevertheless, he wasn't going to let her out of his site for the next twenty-four hours if he could help it. "It's writing as we speak, isn't it?!" he persisted. Indeed, even as he pointed it out, the swirls and scribbles continued to multiply at the base of the screen.

"I know. They are. It is." She stumbled. "But only certain angels have access to that much information."

"And you're not one of them?" Alter goaded.

"No," she confirmed forlornly.

"Because?" he pushed her.

"Of you," she mumbled to his surprise.

"What?" he almost yelled, only half certain of what she had just said.

"Because of you," she repeated, raising her own voice to match him.

"What about me?" he protested.

She sighed once more. "I think the exact words were: "If we gave you the keys to the Kingdom of Heaven you'd only pass them over to that Demon.""

Alter thought about this for a moment, unsure quite how to react to this useful piece of information. "Is that true?" he asked hopefully.

"Yes," she answered unhappily.

"You'd really give me the keys to Heaven?"

"No!" she objected, realising what he had meant. "I'm not allowed those either, thanks to you. I'm one of the few angels who still has to knock, *thanks to you*." Despite the echoes to her prose, he was unmoved and not in the least bit guilty about the predicament he was apparently responsible for putting her in. In fact, he was positively amused by it all.

"Are you the *only* one?" he niggled at her. Morana stayed silent, refusing to allow him to get to her - or at least to show him that he had. Her silence said enough, and he turned away from her to stifle a laugh. When he turned back, however, he was grave-faced once more. "So, what are we going to do about this missing soul and body then?"

"I don't know."

Not for the first time, they both thought hard about the situation, and not for the first time, neither of them could come up with a sensible solution.

"Shall we sleep on it and come back tomorrow?" he suggested.

"Yeah, OK," she readily agreed. And so they both gave up, and made to leave the missing dead man's house. But not before Morana had sneaked the laptop behind her back, cleverly concealing it beneath her wing feathers.

"Yeah. It'll be nice to have a day off for a change," Alter said, wandering casually back to the coffee table. "I'm just going to get another one of those biscuits and I'll be right with you," he lied. Instead of the plate of biscuits, he nimbly reached for the autobiography, slipping the whole thing beneath his jacket where it somehow disappeared without a lump of a trace, then made his way calmly back to the front door to meet up with the angel. Although, halfway there, he changed his mind and popped back for the biscuits after all...

Private Investigations

They barely spoke of the case of the missing cadaver on their return, and chose instead to go their separate ways, both feigning the need for rest and relaxation. Neither left the house, staying alert of the other, just in case they might try to.

Later that evening, Morana was sat in the dark at the kitchen table in her comfortable jersey pyjamas, the laptop open and glowing against her face. The annotated picture of the dead actor was displayed before her, held to the fridge door by two magnets - one a chubby angel, one a classical devil depiction. The only other light source was coming through the kitchen door from the hallway. She stared blankly at the screen, unable to concentrate.

Alter walked in, so engrossed in reading the large book in his hands he was totally oblivious to Morana's presence. He turned on the light, making the angel blink uncomfortably. He walked to the fridge and acknowledged the photo stuck to it with a friendly tip of the head.

"Will," he greeted it, before opening the fridge door and taking out a beer, his eyes permanently fixed to the words on the page before him. He laughed out loud as he closed the fridge door and shook his head at the photo staring back. "What a cock," he declared. He turned around and nearly jumped out of his simulated skin at the sight of Morana watching his moves with captivated amusement. He quickly recovered his composure and eyed her suspiciously. "Still up then?"

"Yes," she replied just as cagily, wincing as his eyes fell upon the laptop.

"What are you doing?" He marched around the table to take a closer look, but she turned the screen away from him before he got there.

"Playing chess?" she lied unconvincingly, immediately feeling bad for doing so, and then realising her mistake as the look of excitement crossed his face.

"Ooh, can I-?"

"No!" she interrupted before he could make her dishonesty any worse. His suspicion grew at her refusal, but he walked away nonetheless, and took a seat opposite her.

"Isn't that Bailey's book?" she asked, pointing to the mound of paper in his hand. He looked up guardedly.

"Isn't that Bailey's laptop?" he accused back, but they knew they had both been found out. "Why don't we pool resources? Compare notes?" he suggested sagely. "What have you found out?"

"The refresh button might be broken," she groaned. "It keeps crashing on me." This was not the answer he had been hoping for.

"How are you connected to the internet anyway? I didn't know this place was wireless?"

"Oh, no, it's not. I'm using this." Morana tapped a black box, which had been plugged into the back of the laptop since she'd brought it home. "AUM." He looked questioningly at her and she explained, "Automatic Universal Matrix. It's a server interface block... thingie. Connects directly up," she quoted, pointing upwards as if to clarify the point. "Omnipresent Internet Anywhere."

Alter grimaced at her need for commercialising, yet couldn't help being mildly impressed. "I must say, you guys are definitely coming on in the technology stakes. Although I have noticed you're still using PC plods."

"Bill Gates has done Him a lot of favours recently," she confided. "Anyway, what's wrong with PCs?" she contended. "What else would you use?"

Alter smiled mischievously, picking up an apple from the purely decorative fruit bowl that sat in the centre of the table. "Apples have been working for us since the year dot," he winked, taking a bite before remembering he wasn't that keen on Grannies. He screwed his face up and threw the uneaten fruit away. Morana shook her head regrettably at the wastage. "Anyway, back to Bailey," he declared.

"Right," she agreed.

"We're looking for a man," he stated.

"Right," she repeated.

"Raised by an actress and a lion tamer."

"Right." She stopped and thought about his words for a split second. "What? Is that what it says in there?" she giggled, incredulously tapping at the autobiography.

"Why? What does yours say?"

Morana briefly scanned some of the earlier records. "I think it does mention his mother was an amateur actress. His dad worked at London Zoo for a bit."

"Did his dad work with the lions?"

"He might have done," she conceded. "I don't know. I'm not looking at his dad's record. Do you want me to?"

He thought about it, but shook his head. "No. Not important. Let's stick to what we need to know. Where was he last?" He checked his own source with a little more reservation this time. "According to the last few pages of the biog here, he's on a high, doing pretty well for himself, looking forward to the film industry's criticisms of his latest film, blah blah blah, and, would you believe it? He thinks he deserves a holiday." He looked up for any comment from Morana, but she was still busy searching her own notes. "Maybe he's dead in the middle of the ocean on some fancy yacht, or in some secluded chateaux or beach house? Maybe we were just sent to the wrong place? It's all been a total admin balls up."

"No, he's nowhere near a beach, and he is..." she paused with a sudden surprised realisation. "He is still alive... Or he was, twelve hours ago." They sat in silence for a moment, taking in this surreal information.

"How is that possible?" Alter finally broke the hush.

"It says here," Morana explained from the Akashik record, "that he was taken ill five months ago. Collapsed at a party. He - and everyone else - thought it was a little too much revelry, but test results showed it to be more serious. He was diagnosed with hepatic tumours. Liver cancer. Terminal, poor chap. They put him on the donor list, but were always doubtful, even if one was found in time, that he'd survive an operation. The cancer's growing too quickly. After a couple of painful bouts of chemo, he decided to defy everyone, keep it all to himself and quit everything. He jetted off to the Peruvian rainforest for some fresh air. It seems he may have got the idea that he'd find a cure for cancer there too."

"Foolish mankind," Alter interrupted dismissively. "Always looking for things in the wrong places."

"He went out trekking by himself," she continued, "and then..."

"What? He's dead in the jungle?" he asked sarcastically.

"No, I told you he's not dead! He just... met a man."

"Who, Tarzan?"

Morana frowned at Alter's aggravation, but she couldn't blame him for it. The story was sounding more absurd, even in the true records.

"Some old man. It's just..."

"What?"

"Well..." she hesitated. "This man was either a witch doctor or a scientist... The symbol for him isn't in First Angelics. For some reason, it's in a much older language form. But it looks like the symbol for a type of doctor..." She screwed her eyes up as she stared at the image on the screen, as if looking at it through a slit might make sense of it...

"It just doesn't make sense," she finally declared.

"Does it matter?" he asked irritably. "He got lost in the jungle and met an old man. Is the old man going to kill him?"

"No. Well, no, I don't know. Not exactly." Alter rolled his eyes and Morana returned to the translation. "He gave Bailey a packet of some sort of powder. It says here the man spoke in a language Bailey clearly understood, and he seemed to understand Bailey perfectly well too. Which is odd, don't you think?" She looked at Alter who shrugged and motioned for her to continue with a brusque roll of his hand. "The man was living in some sort of shelter in the forest - a cross between a tepee and a tent. He appeared from out of nowhere, beckoned Bailey in and gave him the powder. He told Bailey to mix a spoonful into his drinks every morning and evening and his life would be prolonged."

"Sounds unlikely," Alter scoffed. "Are you sure you're not on Wikipedia by mistake?"

Morana ignored him, continuing to paraphrase the page. "He put some of the powder in their drinks there and then, so Bailey would trust him. They drank together and Bailey was stunned by how much better he instantly felt. Very alive and energetic. He began to really believe the old man's claims and, of course, thought he had stumbled on the cure for cancer after all. Like this was all predestined."

"Very unlikely!" Alter jeered. "Typical actor, always has to be the hero of everything. And how can that possibly be the cure? You know as well as I do that it's not in the bloody rainforest!"

"Yes, I know. But still…" Morana was only half listening to his protests. "The records show that, whatever the powder was, it *is* having an effect."

"What's in it then?"

"Hang on." Morana clicked on the symbol for the old man, expecting it to open up a new record for this obscure stranger. The coloured bar gradually lengthened across the bottom of the page while the two users watched with baited breath. Eventually, just as they were about to give up, the page loaded with the ominous words: "Access Denied: Level 7 Clearance Only".

"What?" Alter stepped back irritably.

"This is all too weird," Morana shook her head, slightly afraid of what they had got themselves into.

"What??" Alter repeated with just a touch more irritation.

"The old man," she explained. "He's a complete enigma. He appears from out of nowhere, speaks clear English, or clear something anyway, and seems to possess the elixir of life. And yet... he doesn't exist."

"What do you mean, he doesn't exist?" her demon housemate ordered, crossing his arms with exasperation. Morana tapped the screen's forbidding words. "Can't you get Level 7 clearance from someone?"

"No, that's my point," she whined. "Hardly anyone has Level 7 access."

"Are you sure it's not just you again?" he mockingly challenged.

"Not this time," she answered with deadpan earnest, causing an ancient, instinctive fear to rise within Alter.

"Well, what do you have?" he asked a little more cautiously.

"Level 2." She hesitated. "Sort of." She hesitated again. "It's user defined," she added, feebly attempting to cover her inadequacies. She had felt so good when she'd showed him this site at Bailey's house, so capable and clever. She'd completely forgotten just how much trouble she'd got herself into over him.

Alter was no longer interested in her lack of competence, however. He wanted answers to this growing mystery and he didn't have the patience for all these hold-ups.

"So how *do* we find out what's going on?"

"We don't," she answered dolefully. "At least not from here." She flipped back to Bailey's page and read a little more from his record. "The old man hid the powder in a statue of some local god. He then led Bailey back to a main road with many words of wisdom. Or something. Bailey found himself surprisingly close to his hotel."

"Waking up in his own bed just in time to discover it was all a dream," Alter ridiculed.

"It doesn't say that," she dismissed him, but double-checked the page, just to be sure. "But it *is* all too... unbelievable."

"He is an actor," Alter reasoned.

"Yes, but this is supposed to be his life. His real, actual life. And it all just sounds too..." Morana twirled her fingers in the air trying to think of another word for unbelievable. When, after five seconds, she still hadn't produced one, Alter's impatience snapped back into place.

"So what happened next? Where is he now?"

"OK, OK," she tried to calm him. "Well..." she scrolled further down the life story. "He got stopped by customs on his return-"

"Aha! Jail," Alter interrupted.

"No."

"What?" he cried in disbelief.

"They searched his bag and found the statue, but didn't open it. It just appeared to be solid to them."

"Or maybe they didn't *try* to open it?" he argued, disappointed.

"Either way, he got to his rented penthouse in London without anyone questioning the powder. And the statue opened easily when he tried it."

"How nice," Alter mused sarcastically.

"And he's been using it ever since," she added, continuing to read.

"Which is how long?"

"Four days now. If he keeps using the powder the way he is, he'll have used it up by this time next week." She read a little more to herself and frowned. "He's so convinced it's curing him, he's made an appointment for a scan. At St George's Hospital. He's getting the powder analysed and-"

"When?" Alter interjected excitedly.

"What? Oh. Tomorrow." She looked at her housemate's suddenly glinting eyes and curling smile. For once he was ready to be patient, but tense, as he allowed her a few moments to acknowledge what she had just discovered. "Tomorrow!" she yelled as soon as she understood, and Alter finally felt able to relax and enjoy the moment. "At nine! That's it!"

"We've got him," he joined in, salivating at the thought of that soul finally becoming his, before noticing the angel's raised eyebrow. "I mean, found him," he quickly corrected.

They smiled at each other with the mutual satisfaction of a job well done. Alter motioned to the computer, and Morana waited for the plan, the useful piece of information, the praise of her work - anything that would continue this moment of cooperation between them.

"Can I play chess now?" he asked.

The Miracle Cure

The following morning, still unable to completely trust each other, they travelled to St George's Hospital together to search for the undead man and his sought-after soul. Hairs stood on end on the napes of necks and many a spine tingled with discomfort as they wandered about the hospital, remaining imperceptible by all but those few unfortunate people on the brink of crossing over to the other side, who eyed them with a mixture of fear and awe. Having searched a few wards and peered over the shoulders of a few receptionists, Morana and Alter were beginning to grow weary of the whole episode. They slumped down onto the only spare adjacent seats in the A&E waiting room.

Alter checked his PDA hopefully, but those hopes were quickly dashed by the view on the screen.

"Damn it," he cursed. "Still the only appointment."

"Have you checked with your appointments administrators?" Morana suggested.

"No time to," he dismissed her.

"Really?" She was surprised, as he usually had a way of making time for anything and everything, something she couldn't help admiring, though she was forever in the dark as to how he managed it.

"This is an important job, Angel," he snapped. "Apparently." It was certainly true he'd been told so, but he could not understand why he was being made to chase after the living when there were so many potential souls to steal right in front of him.

"OK," Morana relented. She looked about them, baffled as to how they were going to get this job done - whatever this job really was. "I guess we need to find a way to infiltrate. Get close to the man. Find out what he knows."

"Alright, Miss Marple!" he joked, although he was secretly pleased for the boost of enthusiasm. And it couldn't have been better timed, for just at that moment two nurses passed their seats, giggling and whispering in an unmistakeable way. The seated two turned to follow the path of their interest and there, at the end of the corridor, was Wilfred Bailey Jr. Morana threw her arm across Alter's chest and pushed him back in what would have been a covert way, had they not been sat in the open.

"There he is!" she whispered loudly. He frowned back at her, lowering her arm from his chest and wondering how she could change so quickly and imperviously from impressive to ridiculous.

"Why are we hiding in the middle of a room from someone who can't see us, isn't looking for us, and has no idea who we are?" he asked, crossing his arms and making her feel as stupid as he thought of her right then.

"I don't know. I'm just nervous," she whimpered. "I've rarely dealt with the living before. They all seem a bit-"

"Stupid?" he offered.

"Complicated," she corrected.

"They're easy," he attempted to reassure her. "You just tell them what they want to hear and they'll do anything you ask."

"But how do we get close to him?" It seemed a strange question to ask, since they were an angel and a demon, both perfectly capable of being visible or imperceptible by choice. But this was an odd situation. At some point, they both knew, they were going to have to interact with Bailey to uncover the truth. And there was no time like the present.

And as Alter watched the streams of staff and patients file past them, he realised there was no better answer to her query than: "Subterfuge."

⏳

Not long after his inspiration, Morana found herself standing outside a door marked Private, which lead into a staff area. She was dressed in a simple nurse's uniform and shuffling uncomfortably. Alter stepped out of the door wearing the garb of a doctor, complete with a badge stating him to be 'Chief Surgeon'.

He looked Morana up and down. "Nice," he concluded in a tone she didn't entirely approve of and chose to ignore.

"He went in there," she gestured towards Radiology.

Rather helpfully, the Radiology suite had a nice clean window, behind which stood the disguised angel and demon, watching Bailey reappear from a full-body scanner. The dashing actor was being helped up by a blushing nurse, while a doctor checked the resulting scan images with a heavy frown and a rub of the chin. Bailey smiled nervously as the nurse ushered him through to a comfortable chair in the small consultation room next-door. She poured out and offered him a glass of mineral water, which he accepted politely. She leant over as she handed it to him, in the kind of provocative way that made Alter feel proud. Morana glanced across at her demonic companion to make sure he was not in some way influencing the scene, but he gave nothing away with his usual smirk; the frisson of sexual tension between the nurse and patient was far too obvious for him. Before Morana had a chance to insult Alter by asking him about her suspicions, their flirtation was interrupted by the entrance of the still-frowning doctor.

"I'm pleased to hear that your vacation was beneficial." He spoke in a tone that suggested the worse and the nurse quickly excused herself, returning to the scanning room to tidy up. Alter watched her intensely, her blushed cheeks and filthy imaginings she thought no one else could see. He recognised a kindred soul. Morana chose to ignore his new project, and stayed with the investigation.

"Was I right?" Bailey was asking the doctor, whose frown was becoming a permanent feature across his forehead.

"Psychologically speaking, you appear immensely improved, Mr Bailey."

"Wilfred, please," the patient offered, and the doctor smiled, briefly displaying a smoother face. He hesitated, the familiarity making him even more uncomfortable with the truth.

"I'm sorry to say so," he apologised, "but it appears that is the only noticeable improvement. The scans show..." he paused unhappily, double-checking the images and figures as if expecting them to have changed in the last thirty seconds, "no improvement in the number of tumours."

Bailey silently contemplated this for a moment. "Are you sure?" he asked in a voice that croaked a little, causing him to reach quickly for his glass of water. He took a sip as the doctor and Morana looked on sympathetically. "I mean, really sure?"

"This is my analysis, based on your scan results," the doctor confirmed. "I am happy to arrange for them to be sent to another specialist for a second opinion, of course."

"But it doesn't make any sense!" Bailey snapped with frustration, his face visibly pained by the bad news.

"I'm afraid," the doctor spoke in a calming voice, "no matter how good the Peruvian air might be in the jungle-"

"It's not that," Bailey interrupted. The doctor sat back in his own chair thoughtfully. He was aware that something strange was going on with his famous patient, but had yet to receive an inkling of what.

Death By Chocolate
―――――――――

"Can I ask what it is that made you so certain of an improvement?"

"It was nothing, clearly," Bailey answered in a quiet voice, tinged with genuine confusion. It was a confusion Morana could completely understand. If the old man's powder wasn't making him physically better, then what was it doing to help him?

"Your general health does seem remarkably improved," the doctor added, choosing not to pry further into his patient's confidentiality, hoping positivity might clear the mystery up. "You're far more energetic than I would have expected from a man at such advanced stages - particularly after such a physically and mentally demanding vacation. I have no doubt your positive and relaxed attitude is making you feel so much better, and I can only encourage this, of course." There was little doubt the doctor was wondering if this 'positive and relaxed attitude' was really due to some unprescribed narcotic, but he was not prepared to ask outright and lose his profitable patient.

Bailey was certainly not ready to admit to some placebo he'd picked up in foreign climes. "I'm grateful to you for obliging me in this," he concluded, holding out his hand to the doctor who shook it willingly.

"Not at all, Mr-" he stopped himself short with a smile of a self-reminder, "Wilfred. I welcome any possibility of a cure, I assure you. If I had noticed even the slightest improvement I would have packed as many of my clients as possible off to Peru," he joked benignly and Bailey smiled in acknowledgement, though he still could not disguise his heavy disappointment. "It grieves me not to be able to give you better news," the doctor added, and Bailey nodded sadly. "If you'll follow me to the private waiting room," he said, standing, emphasising 'private' as if it were the greatest perk the hospital could offer him, "I'll be along shortly to discuss your continuing medication and confirm your next appointment." The sound of his suddenly cheerier voice called the nurse to wake from her disturbing daydreams. She pulled herself together and returned to the two gentlemen, flushed and smiling, hoping they'd see her reddened cheeks as a sign of hard work and nothing more. She ushered Bailey out of the room on cue, unable to look him in the eye this time.

Morana and Alter, their faces stuck against the window, watched the party leave; the angel observing with pity, while the demon looked pleasantly confused. They peeled their faces away from the pane.

"It doesn't make any sense," Morana verbalised what they were both thinking. "Why hasn't the powder made him better?"

"Why would we still be here if it had?" Alter replied sensibly, sneaking a surreptitious glance at his PDA screen and grimacing at the lack of change.

"Oh yeah," Morana agreed airily. "But what was the point in it all then? Why the Peruvian powder and the strange old man?"

"Who knows?" he answered seriously. "But we need to get a look at those test results. And I want to know exactly what's in that powder." He marched after the doctor and patient, leaving Morana behind.

"Why?" She called, chasing after him for a reply that wasn't coming...

Mind Tricks

Morana caught up with Alter outside the waiting room door. He was about to knock, and Morana's heart raced with anticipation - faking humanity was nearly the most terrifying thing she had done that week, just beaten by the harvesting of numerous murdered souls... But before his fist had reached the wood, Bailey's doctor returned, clipboard and file in hand. Alter smiled casually at the man, while Morana cowered just behind the demon. The doctor frowned at the pair, and in particular at the fact that they were blocking his way. He opened his mouth to speak, but was pre-empted by Alter.

"Do you mind if I take a look at that?" he asked, reaching out for the clipboard. The doctor's spine tensed with suspicions, and Morana held her breath.

"Of course I mind!" he retorted angrily, pulling the clipboard sharply out of reach. "Who are you? I don't know you. Are you press or something? I'll call security. Of course you can't look at this. This is private." He spoke so fast that Alter had absolutely no hope of getting a word in edgeways. But even the threat of security was not enough to scare the demon, who decided to resort to a form of good old-fashioned persuasion. He stared hard into the doctor's eyes and, although he didn't need to do it - he just liked the effect - he flickered his fingers about the doctor's face.

"Actually, I *can* take a look at it," Alter calmly commanded. The doctor froze, mildly mesmerised by the fingers flitting in and out of his eye line.

"Actually, you *can* take a look at it," he mimicked hesitantly, gradually handing the clipboard over to the demon, unable to comprehend why he should be doing so.

"In fact, it would probably be best if *I* read the results to the patient," Alter continued, prising the clipboard carefully out of his hands.

"It probably would be best if you did," the doctor agreed, still with some uncertainty to his voice.

"And then you can go for a coffee and Danish in the canteen," Alter guided him.

"I do really fancy a coffee and Danish, but-"

"Good man." Alter patted the doctor's shoulder and, before the man could wake from his stupor, turned him around with a gentle shove in what he hoped was the direction of the canteen. As the doctor shuffled away, Alter congratulated himself on a job well done and turned to Morana for likewise praise, only to find her glaring back at him, arms crossed and foot angrily tapping the ground.

"What?" he asked defensively, his face dropping.

Death By Chocolate

"You can't do that," she objected.

"What?" he repeated, knowing full well.

"Influence free will!"

Alter couldn't help himself. He wafted his fingers in front of her eyes, tightly held her gaze and pronounced: "I think you'll find I *can*."

Predictably, but for Alter still a little disappointingly, Morana was totally unaffected by his mind tricks.

"No you *can't*," she announced angrily. Alter huffed sulkily.

"You heard the man - he really wanted a Danish!" But his defence produced a further harsh look from his companion, and he lowered his head to the clipboard like an admonished schoolboy, trying to work out how she always managed to make him feel bad about doing what he felt to be right. "You're just jealous 'cause *you* can't do it," he moped. And then he realised something about her abilities. Something so important that-

"What's on the chart?" she interrupted his train of thought. He looked up at her expectant face and just for a moment they both felt the power shift between them... His mind momentarily dissolved as he gazed blankly into her eyes. She motioned helpfully towards the clipboard, and he recovered his reason, flipping quickly through the notes, stopping now and then to read a word or two. Then he flipped through a little more slowly, reading a few more words. He looked up at Morana.

"Nothing."

"Nothing?" she repeated.

"Nothing," he confirmed. He turned and reached for the door handle, but Morana stopped him before he could turn it, their hands intermingling on the knob.

"What are you going to say?" she asked urgently.

"Nothing," he shrugged. They froze for a moment, Alter looking at Morana, waiting for something to make sense...

And then she realised what it was he wanted, and apologetically let go of his hand.

Death By Chocolate

Waiting For...

It certainly was a private waiting room - only two, comfortable leather chairs, a lovely picture of a peaceful English meadow (to make up for the lack of a window, itself a deterrent to press-spies and fanatic stalkers), and a little table, decorated with a vase of flowers - daisies and tulips, Morana noted - as well as some more of that expensive bottled water and clean, crystal glasses. While Morana took in the scene, Wilfred Bailey Jr was startled and a little unnerved by the two strangers who had just entered. Alter smiled reassuringly at him; Bailey felt anything but reassured - in fact, as the two of them looked down on him, he had the strangest sensation someone had just walked over his grave.

Everyone seemed to be waiting for someone else to speak, and soon Bailey's expectancy turned from curiosity to mild impatience at their silence.

"Is something wrong?" he asked, beginning to suspect these two were just fans who had managed to commandeer a couple of fake uniforms for the privilege of meeting him; something he was only half annoyed about.

"With what?" Alter replied vaguely. Bailey looked at him distrustfully.

"With my results?" he answered, indicating the clipboard in the almost certainly fake doctor's hand.

Alter laughed flamboyantly at his own apparent foolishness, then snapped quickly out of it. "Should there be something wrong?" He raised his eyebrow inquisitively at the actor, who was no longer sure whether to laugh or call for help.

"Who are you?" he demanded.

"I'm your doctor," Alter answered calmly.

"No you're not," Bailey rejected with certainty. Alter lifted one hand from the clipboard and stepped a little closer to his victim, beginning to wave his fingers about the man's face.

"Don't," came a hissed female warning in his right ear. Alter dropped his hand despondently and scowled back at Morana before returning happily to the patient.

"No, you're right, I'm not. But I am *a* doctor," he lied, "and I have been working on your case."

"Then why have I never met you before?" Bailey probed. Before Alter could answer, the actor pointed to his nametag. "Aren't you a surgeon? My condition is supposedly inoperable now; my *real* doctor told me so. Why would I need a surgeon?"

Alter casually sat down in the only other free chair and smiled. "These are all good questions," he agreed. "Nurse?" Morana started, realising he meant her, though he wasn't looking her way, his gaze firmly on Bailey.

"What?" she asked, shuffling herself over to the other side of Bailey, so the poor actor felt completely pinned in by the strange pair. Alter's eyes flitted from her to the patient, commanding her to say something. "Erm… Look… The thing is, we can't find anything wrong with you-" (Alter coughed.) "I mean, right with you-" she corrected, but again Alter warned her with another clearing of his throat, "I mean…" she panicked desperately, "different about you since the last visit?" Alter slumped back in his chair with an anguished sigh. "Perhaps you could help us a little by telling us what's been going on. Have you been… taking anything unusual?" The demon shook his head. It was like training a novice. He made a mental note never again to go on an investigative mission with an angel; honesty and decency were not the right job specifications.

Her question made Bailey flinch. Maybe the traces of powder in his blood samples had given him away? What if the lab had discovered it was something illegal? Perhaps they weren't fans at all, but some sort of undercover narcotics police? If that were true, he couldn't let them know he was on to them. He'd played a similar role before, in that film, Havana Raiders. He'd won an Oscar for that, so he must have been good. All he had to do was deflect his fears.

"Are you a… psychiatrist?" he asked Morana as she smiled hopefully down at him. From the moment she'd sat next to him, he'd wondered about telling her everything. She seemed somehow sympathetic. Yet he couldn't help but feel the eyes of that fake surgeon burrowing into him from the other side and was determined not to give in.

"Not that I know of," she answered placidly, sensing his disquiet. "We're just concerned for your well-being. Some people find that a change in routine helps to distract them or increase positive feeling when going through difficult times."

Her words sounded sensible. He looked at her, and just for a moment he could feel himself wanting to confess to her, everything he had ever done wrong, no matter what the consequences might be. The chair next to his squeaked eagerly.

"It doesn't matter," he dismissed his thoughts and the strangers' anticipation. "Thank you for your time. I'm just sorry it was wasted."

"No," Morana began to protest, but Bailey was already on his feet and she and Alter reluctantly saw him out of the room. "If you should need to talk to someone...?" she called after him, but he disappeared with a grateful smile.

"He's right, you do sound like a psychiatrist," Alter said as they watched him leave. "And you're about as much use." Morana grimaced, reluctant to openly lay blame on her demonic companion for their failed first contact. Bailey seemed to have a far greater notion of who they really were than he was letting on.

Watching The Detectives

Dealing with the living was a tiring task. That evening they slumped at the kitchen table, exhausted, still wearing the stolen uniforms, deep in thought over their next move; how they might solve this case and get on with their day jobs, so to speak.

Alter rubbed his eyes and stared at the ceiling. Morana rested her head in her hands. She sighed heavily and slowly fell back into her chair.

"Anything?" Alter asked.

"Still nothing," she replied regretfully.

"Bloody hell!" he cursed angrily, making her jump. "This is detective work! This is not what I signed up for," he moaned.

"Actually, I'm quite enjoying it," she reasoned a little more cheerfully.

"Fine. You do it. You find out what's going on here," he griped.

"Alright! Calm down." She frowned, concerned by how much this had got to him. It was true they seemed to be no further forward in understanding what was going on than they had been at Bailey's house, but she felt confident there must still be a reason why they had both been asked to do this, and that reason, therefore, must be within their grasp. Well, *fairly* confident...

"Sorry," he brooded. "I'm just sick of having to put my entire existence on hold while this guy is being so... alive!" Morana nodded consolingly. "Everything's suddenly about him! How? Why? What is going on?" Alter beat his hands down on the table with frustration, then covered his face with them.

"Shall I get us some cake?"

Alter could feel the fury growing. This was her answer to everything - food! Drink! A nice cup of bloody Earl Grey and a slice of Battenburg! He threw his hands in the air.

"No! I don't-" he began to yell at her, but the sight of her hang-dog face cooled his temper a little. "I just want to know. There's nothing here," he added, pulling the medical clipboard out from under the table and slamming it down on the wood. She'd completely forgotten he even had that.

"Shouldn't you have given that back?" she asked sensibly.

"I couldn't remember where to put it," he confessed, and before she had time to make any further suggestions, he touched it gently with a fingertip. Its edges slowly folded in on themselves, turning black, until it dissolved into a pile of ash. Morana shook her head with a frown but decided it wasn't a good idea to reprimand him in his current mood. She stood up instead and made her way to the fridge.

"It doesn't make any sense," Alter continued his complaints as she busied herself about the largely empty shelves. "You can't find out anything from that thing," he pointed at the stolen laptop, which now balanced precariously on top of the wastepaper basket where he'd thrown it in an earlier rage. "Nothing about the old man's powder; none of the hospital or lab tests have given anything away. Bailey-boy's saying nothing. Yet it's the only possible reason for his continuing to be a bane on my bloody personal organiser!" He threw the said PDA at the bin and Morana, foreseeing the inevitable destruction, willed it to miss the laptop by inches. She still hoped to return the computer to its rightful owner in one piece one day, having never felt good about the theft in the first place, but especially not once she'd discovered the owner was still alive. She grimaced guiltily at his ruined photograph on the fridge door, then returned to the table with a large chunk of chocolate cake.

"Maybe it's not about the powder after all?" she suggested nonchalantly, chomping at a large forkful of sweet, gooey crumbliness. Alter watched her with an air of disbelief. He waited a few seconds for her to elucidate, but she carried on eating and smiling at him.

"Then *what*?" he exploded, causing her fork to squeak noisily against the china plate. "What? What is the point? What? The man is supposed to be dead!"

Morana looked up from her dessert, determined to stay calm in the face of his outbursts. And nothing was going to ruin her enjoyment of a good piece of cake.

"Only according to our personal organisers," she pointed out placidly. "The Akashik records quite clearly state he's alive and should remain so for several days."

"You're saying you think it's an administration error after all?" Alter perked up, sensing a possible way out of the problem at last.

"I'm just saying," she swallowed and scraped at the leftover frosting, "we never really did look into that possibility. Not properly." She licked her fork pleasurably. "And we do seem to have exhausted the powder theory for now. We know it's the only thing keeping him alive, although he doesn't have an ever-lasting supply. Maybe we were just sent too early?" She dropped her fork back onto the empty plate, suddenly realising she was speaking more sense than she'd expected. "We just need to make sure there wasn't a mistake. Someone might have got the date wrong and we're really due next week?"

"Or maybe one of my bastard colleagues is putting me off the scent to get his own targets up?" Alter added, finally happy with the way this investigation was going. This was something they could rectify, something they could work out!

"There you go!" Morana was pleased to see her housemate returning to his collected self. "Or maybe you're being punished for helping me?" Her suggestion was meant to be just another detached thought for them to consider, and yet they both paused uneasily.

"Right," Alter announced before the tension could become unbearable, "you go your way, I'll go mine. Let's meet back here at, say, morning?"

Before she could answer, he was out of the door and on his way to the bowels of Hell. She screwed her face up. Morning was not good for her at all...

Emma Walker

The First Circle

Alter found his way to the dingy, cellar-like office of the administrators. Harsh fluorescent over-head lights reflected against anti-morale posters on the walls, and showed up the brown and grey tobacco-smoke-stained ceiling. Another demon sat at a computer desk, relaxing back into his office chair, wearing what may once have been a smart, red-tinged suit, scuffed fur loafers and no socks. Alter grimaced at his unkempt appearance, but such was the way with these office dogs.

"Sorry mate, no can do," was his contrary reply to Alter's request for a change of clients. "He's officially yours."

"He's not dead!" Alter pointed out irritably.

The office demon sat up and flexed out his under-used fingers. "That's your problem, not mine. Can't you tempt him into it?"

"It *is* your problem if there's been an admin cock-up," Alter growled.

"There hasn't," he was answered resolutely.

Death By Chocolate

"Have you checked?"

"Yes."

"Can I?" Alter's question was more of a command, and he reached for the demon's computer.

"No!" the office demon yelled, beginning to feel riled, protectively twisting the screen away from his unwanted intruder.

Alter stared at him in disbelief. Conversing with office demons was like trying to make a deal with a brick wall. Their only agenda was to support whomever was above them at all times whilst staying in one piece. He needed to break through somewhere, aim from a different angle.

"Who's covering my rounds while this bloody balls-up of yours continues?"

The office demon scowled at the continued allegation. He tapped a few keys and checked the screen, still making sure Alter couldn't see what was on it. Then he suddenly turned very smugly to his accuser.

"I think it's mostly been passed to Abalam."

"Damn it!" Alter punched the poster to his side, making the office demon scowl as he creased the 'Your Company Loves Misery' slogan. "And damn *you*!"

"Look, I'm telling you, this is not my cock up," the office demon insisted, incensed at the attack on his favourite wall-print. "Everyone else's organisers are working perfectly fine. I've had no other complaints. Abalam is actually receiving all your area deaths as if they were his anyway. It's almost as if you don't exist on the death duty rosters anymore."

"Thanks," Alter replied despondently.

"Are you sure you haven't been fired?" the office demon asked unsympathetically.

"Would I be standing here if I had been?" They both knew being fired from Hell was pretty literal.

"Promotion then?"

"No!"

"Or a punishment?" the office demon continued, still determined to deflect the blame from himself. "It *could* be a punishment?"

"Why, what have you heard?" Alter demanded, his suspicions aroused by the second implication in one night.

"Well," the office demon's haughty smiled returned and he was pleased to see he'd hit a nerve. "There was some rumour about you and this angel - something about you playing away? Cavorting with the enemy?"

"It's not like that," he flouted angrily. "She was the lesser of two evils."

"What?" the office demon looked confused.

"Nothing." Alter realised he'd already been coerced into saying too much. "Look, just get me some other appointments will you."

"Nope. No can do. Sorry mate." It was clear the office demon wasn't the least bit sorry.

"What do you mean 'no can do sorry mate'?" Alter echoed.

"I already told you. It's like you don't exist. I can't access you anymore for appointments. See?" For the first time he turned the VDU towards Alter who greedily took in the display. "Locked out." Alter's name was indeed greyed out; uneditable. "If you're wanting to get back in the game, you'll have to go further down the ladder than me for approval. Or you could just finish this undead bloke off and hope that fixes the glitch?" His sly remark was not without merit, but it did little more than return Alter to the start of the circle.

"Is there anyone I can talk to in this place that actually knows what's going on?"

"Yeah, probably." The office demon took a handful of salted peanuts from a small bowl beside his computer and began a haphazard game of throwing them towards his mouth. Since his visitor refused to take that as a sign to leave, he reached across and deftly liberated a set of laminated sheets from beneath a towering tray of files. "Do you want the phone list?"

Emma Walker

Cloud Eight

Having worked on her nerves with her second piece of cake that evening, Morana finally made the trip up to the lower levels of Heaven. She walked cautiously through the clean, white spaces; simply decorated yet sparkling with beauty. No matter the time of day on earth, heaven was always filled with a warm, golden light. Grand arches broke the wide empty spaces and she could hear the sound of gentle music, the trickling of fountains, and the lively noise of angels chatting and laughing together.

Morana looked hesitantly around, trying to spot someone she knew. She was soon rewarded with the sight of a smiling angel beckoning her, and she slowly traversed the space to the inviting host.

"What are you doing here?" Armatt asked, a tone of friendly concern matching the warm hug she offered and the affectionate looks of those about them.

"Oh. You know." Morana shuffled her feet awkwardly. The rest of the group frowned back, politely awaiting her explanation. "Well, honestly?" They all nodded. "I'm here because... You know Alter?" They didn't respond; merely stared like statues, polite smiles and fretful frowns decorating their carefully chiselled faces. "Alter? The demon I live with?" Morana persisted with her explanation. The gathering looked to each other and back to Morana sympathetically.

"How can you bare to share your space with a demon?" asked Seraph Bagliss, voicing the thoughts of the rest.

"Oh, no, it's fine really," she answered, more than used to this kind of question. "Actually, it's quite convenient. We both like living on the surface - closer to work - and he can do this handy sort of Jedi-mind-trick thing with the landlord and..." She paused at their bewildered looks, some of them desperately biting back any judgements forming in their heads. "Not that I approve of course," she redeemed herself, "but, anyway, he's really not that bad, and-"

"I heard your speech in the Court the other day," the cherub Nem interrupted before she could make things more uncomfortable. "Very thought-provoking."

"Aw, thanks," Morana grinned, while the others looked down at their feet and glanced sideways at each other. "Um, anyway, where was I?" She looked about the small congregation for some indication, but no one came to her aid. She took a deep breath, recalling her last point. "Oh, yeah, he's been - we'll, *we've* been, really - a little worried about this job we've been given. Highly irregular. I mean, we're death wardens, as it were, and yet we're stuck on a job for the living! Which *I'm* fine with, although I don't understand what I'm doing, but Alter, bless him, is a little uneasy about it all..."

The sympathetic smiles returned to their faces, but Armatt excused herself from the rest of the group, taking Morana with her. They moved away to the audible sound of sighs of relief.

"We can't help you," Armatt whispered once they were safely out of earshot of anyone else in the space.

"What?" Morana looked at her with a smile of disbelief, but her companion's face remained earnest. "Oh." She looked at the floor despondently. "Why? Because he's a demon?"

"No, we can't help *you*," the angel clarified.

"Oh. But... that's unusual." Morana had never expected a refusal of help from the Heavenly realms.

"I know. You know we'd really love to. But this is..." the angel looked about them cagily before leaning into Morana conspiratorially. "This is something else. All I can say is, listen to your hunches and go with them. We're all behind you."

"Oh." Morana looked behind her to see the group she had just left waving and offering positive smiles and thumbs up. "That's nice," she smiled, wondering how much use their being behind her would be...

Death By Chocolate

Back To Life

As the sun rose quietly the following morning, peeking beneath the kitchen blind, a thin beam of its golden light moved across Morana as she slept uncomfortably on a kitchen chair, her arms acting as a makeshift pillow between her head and the solid wooden table. Alter, who had barely closed his eyes since returning from the office from Hell, stood with his back to his sleeping housemate, leaning his fists against the kitchen top. He reached for the nearest knife, pulled it out of its wooden storage block and gripped it purposefully in his fist. He took a deep breath and stabbed. Stabbed and stabbed, over and over.

Pieces of Black Forest gateaux stuck to the knife as it sliced and squelched in and out of the cake. Cherry jam oozed from its wounds while cream and chocolate shards flipped across the work surface. He paused, momentarily satisfied by the mess. The room was silent, except for the breathing of the victim's owner against the kitchen table.

Two PDAs bleeped at exactly the same moment. The sudden loud noise shattered the peace. Morana woke with a start, throwing back her head and gripping the edge of the table; Alter dropped the knife with a loud clatter of metal on granite. They reached for their organisers; Morana tiredly, Alter excitedly, still hopeful that the office idiot had worked out the glitch in the system and he might finally have his regular work back. But both screens showed the same appointment. Morana groaned, returning her head to the table. Alter vented his frustration on the PDA by turning it to ash. Just as he'd expected, another instantly appeared, the appointment flashing brightly on its fresh screen. He picked it up angrily and buried it deep within the smashed cake. The sponge glowed red and began to simmer.

Morana lifted up her head and sniffed the air, a strange and disturbing smell of burning cake filling her nostrils. Alter had sat down opposite her, ignoring the smouldering mound behind him. He looked hard at her, desperation swirling through his eyes.

"What are we going to do?" he yowled.

"What's burning?" she asked distractedly.

"Nothing," he replied sheepishly. "What are we going to do?"

"About what?" she yawned. He didn't need to remind her. That very moment their PDAs bleeped again, the noise painfully splitting the air. "Oh. That."

Just behind Alter, part of the gateaux fell apart from itself. Morana tried to look around him to see what was going on, but he dodged and blocked her view like an expert. She grimaced suspiciously at him, but gave in to his questioning.

"I don't know," she yawned again, stretching widely. "All I could gather is that we have to see this through."

"But what does that mean?"

"We'll have to work together," she surmised, although she really had as little idea as he did.

"Which is ridiculous!" he yelled. "It's unnatural!"

"It's hardly the first time," she reminded him.

"And isn't that what got us into this mess in the first place?" he reminded her. "Besides, this is different. I know it. I can smell it."

Morana sniffed the air again. She could definitely smell *something*, but Alter was glaring at her expectantly.

"Well, if you don't want to know what I found out-"

"You said you found nothing?"

"Well, I didn't really find anything... definite," Morana admitted. "But there was something."

"That's better than nothing," he acknowledged eagerly. "What?" Morana offered him a teasing smile. She wasn't prepared to lose the upper hand too quickly. "OK. Fine. Work together," he relented. "I'll get you a new cake. Now, what?"

She frowned at his mention of cake, but decided to make the most of his renewed enthusiasm.

"Just that I was told to follow my hunches. So this is what *I* think is going on: You and I broke the rules. We both have superiors who currently doubt our abilities to do our jobs properly. Mine have made that very clear. Yours..." she looked closely at his uncertain face, "well, yours have cut you out of the system, which I'm guessing is the same thing?" He nodded, unhappily accepting the resemblance. "We know Bailey's powder supply is limited, and is unlikely to last him past the week. We know his test results show he should probably be dead already and it's a miracle he isn't. So, my hunch is that you and I are dealing with an arguer. Only he doesn't know it yet. And may be our job is to argue for him until one of us wins?"

"You mean, compete for a living soul?" The idea pleased and intrigued him, though it seemed an unlikely case. "We have different demon ranks for that," he pointed out.

"Well, now you're one of them," she smiled proudly at him. "You've become a tempter; I've become a protector. Quite exciting isn't it!"

"No," he scowled, "it's a lot more work, and a hell of a lot harder. Why do you think I didn't opt for that role in the first place?" Alter thought about the office demon's suggestion of a promotion. It didn't seem at all likely that a promotion would be the result of his recent actions.

"Makes no difference to me how hard it is," Morana shrugged forlornly. "If I succeed, I still get relocated."

"So give up?" he suggested indifferently. He looked at her sad face and a thought of genuine interest occurred to him. "What will happen if you fail?"

"I think," she sighed, "I'm applying for... humanity."

"What!?" Alter recoiled in his chair.

"There's no other option," she explained. "Besides, I like being here, on the surface. And I am getting a little bored of death - especially after last week." Alter smiled to himself again, forgetting for a moment that she was sat right in front of him. He let the smile drop and nodded gravely. "It's been over a century since I started this job and things are changing so much now. Too quickly for me."

"But *human*?" Alter protested. "What about dog or cat or... elephant?"

"No," she waived his ideas away. "Human. I think I need to reconnect with the corporeal. Might make me better at this job, if I ever get it back." She looked at his horrified face and smiled thoughtfully. "I think you should consider it too."

"Consider what?"

"Humanity."

Alter threw his head back in hysterical laughter. "No thank you! It's so constrictive and pointless. I wouldn't fit in."

"I think you'd fit in perfectly!" she argued, before remembering something else. "What do you mean you'll get me a new cake?" He shuffled across in his seat, allowing Morana a clear view of the crumbling cinders of gateaux. She looked disappointedly at him, then walked across to the mess, extracted Alter's singed PDA from the middle (covered in burnt frosting and smeared with scorched chocolate bits) and handed it back to him.

"Thanks," he said taking it between his thumb and forefinger and dropping it on to the table. He looked at the appointment, still displaying itself on the screen. "I've just thought of something," he realised.

"What?" she asked, prodding at her poor, unfortunate cake.

"You still owe me for the past few days. All those extra souls?"

"What?" She turned to look at him incredulously. He wasn't seriously asking for something more in return for terrorising her for an entire week?

"Yeah," he answered, reading her thoughts. "We made a deal. I gave you the souls and you were to give me something in return, to be specified at a later date."

"I'm not sure those were the *exact* terms," she disagreed, trying to remember what had passed between them that night.

"It was implied," he assured her. Then changing tact slightly, he decided to appeal to her good nature. "You'd be doing me a really big favour?"

She looked at him sceptically. "How?"

Alter rubbed his hands together excitedly, and laid out the new rules of the game.

"If I win Bailey-boy's soul," he declared, "you become human - which you were going to do anyway - and then..." he paused for emphasis, "I get your soul."

"What?" Morana stared at him for a moment, trying to take in his proposal.

"I get your soul," he repeated. "To do with whatever I please, throughout your mortal life."

"But..." Morana could not believe her ears. "That's just wrong!"

"It's perfect!" he contended with glee. "Come on. You know how short life is. I'll break you in gently?" She stood without movement until he almost felt uneasy. "I'll leave it with you," he concluded, pushing his chair away and departing for the comfort of the sofa. Morana watched him leave, a wave of sadness and shock washing over her.

Emma Walker

The Deal

Alter was watching the breakfast news as Morana walked into the living room. The screen was a continual rotation of murders, thefts, bombs, and other man-made catastrophes, with reporters doing their level best to ensure the audience was appropriately scared and intimidated. Alter watched intently, suitably impressed. He smiled up at her sullen face, trying not to care about the hurt in her eyes.

"Look, it's not that bad," he consoled her. "You know the actions of the living don't mean very much in the great scheme of things, no matter how bad you are." He turned back to the TV greedily. "It looks like a lot of fun to me. Why live a pure, dull life when you can go crazy and make a name for yourself, eh? I'm almost tempted to apply for humanity after all."

Morana sat down next to her housemate, picked up the remote control and changed channel. A colourful children's' show bounced around the screen and she watched it vacantly. Alter's head span with all the happy vibes and he stole the remote back, flicking through the channels for something they might be able to agree on.

"Then do that," Morana coldly and unexpectedly announced from beside him, her eyes held fast by the flickering TV.

"Do what?" he answered absent-mindedly, concentrating on his channel-hopping.

"Apply for humanity too," she replied in the same formal tone.

"Don't be daft!" He laughed uneasily. "Why would I...?"

"If you win," she explained, "you get my soul. Fine. I guess I have no real choice in that. Maybe I do owe you. Maybe everyone else is right about you being inherently evil and incapable of good." She had been genuinely wounded by his demand. No matter what anyone had ever accused him of, she'd always believed that deep down he was a good being who would be on her side if push came to shove. She had thought his recent behaviour proved her point. Now she had to question the dark side of her friend. "But that all assumes you'll win," she pointed out. "What if I win?" Alter laughed again. "I'm serious!" she protested.

"Of course you are," he patronised her. "I don't know, dear. You can keep your soul?"

"That won't be enough," she declined. "I have superiors too. And they want me to vanquish you."

"Really?" He shuffled uncomfortably on the cushions. "Why haven't you?"

"I..." She wanted to tell him, but something stopped her. If he didn't know by now, then perhaps there was no point in explaining after all. "That's not important right now. But I can't keep bartering with my soul. It's not enough. If *I* win..." she turned to look him straight in the eye, "then you apply for humanity. We *both* do."

"Ridiculous," he scoffed.

"You just said it would be fun," she reminded him.

"Yeah, but I wasn't being serious!"

"What are you afraid of?" she goaded.

"Nothing!" he objected, unable to look her in the eye.

"Are you afraid I'll win?" she teased.

"Of course not!" he rebuffed. "You've got no chance."

"Well then," she declared, turning to face him. "Do we have a deal?"

He stayed quiet for a moment, watching the TV screen without taking in any of the pictures, waiting to see if his silence would make her relent, but she was happy to patiently wait for his decision. He screwed his face up.

"OK!" he relented.

"Shake on it?" she offered her hand and he reluctantly accepted it with a feeble twitch of the wrist. Suddenly Morana felt cheerier, ready to return to their usual banter. "So... Why do you think I've got no chance?"

"Aside from the obvious?" Alter looked at her spirited face and returned to the subject of Wilfred Bailey Jr. "He's a wastrel."

"He's an actor," she disagreed.

"Even worse! Consistent lying! Don't you read the papers?"

"Of course not." She hated them almost as much as the TV news; so full of lies and gossip and sorrow, feeding some part of the human psyche she couldn't quite grasp. "Why?"

"Homework." Alter rose and walked across to the window, ripping open the living room curtains to reveal an unexpected display. The panes were covered in newspaper clippings, tabloid pictures and headlines, showing the worst side of Bailey - and all quite sensational. Morana joined Alter before the exhibit.

"Wilfred Bailey Junior," Alter summarised. "Cad; Rake; Womaniser. Reformed alcoholic. Recovering drug addict. Relapsed, rehabbed. He was caught with a whore and counselled for kleptomania."

He stepped back, allowing Morana to inspect each story as he spoke. The more she read, the more disturbed she felt, until, unable to take anymore, she swung the curtains closed, instantly re-opening them to reveal a pleasant sunny morning view, the clippings all miraculously disappeared. Morana stared into the sun, the full realisation of what she had agreed to hitting home. Despite her best hopes, Bailey was not going to be an easy soul to acquire.

"We'll see," she thought aloud.

The PDAs beeped from inside the kitchen, causing them both to turn with a start.

"Shh...ugar!" Morana moaned.

"Shit!" Alter cursed at the same time. "Plan?" he asked her urgently.

She took a deep breath. "Breakfast," she decided.

Death By Chocolate

Avenging Angels

With breakfast over, Morana brushed her teeth at the bathroom sink, admiring herself in the mirror for a change. She was looking surprisingly tidy. No one was ever completely without hope. The new plan, the agreement, the knowledge that she only had a few days left of her current incarnation; all of this had boosted her self-confidence somehow. And today she was in a playful mood. She had dressed herself in a Sixties-style outfit: white, A-line mini-dress and silver belt.

She bent over the sink to spit out the mouthful of toothpaste. Lifting her head back up she came face to face with an annotated mirror, the message in thick, white and pink-striped gunks reading: "MORANA, WE'RE NEEDED."

Alter walked in carrying a bottle of pink mouthwash. He, too, was dressed even more impressively than usual, in a smart, charcoal and red-tinted suit, topped with a bowler hat. This was now serious business. He poured Morana a cup of the pink liquid and then one for himself. They clinked, drank, gargled the contents about their mouths, and spat together into the sink. Smiling, Alter gestured for

Morana to depart first with a flourish of his hat, and she graciously accepted. He flipped his hat back on and followed her.

Outside the front door, Morana and Alter admired the morning, each other and their new sense of purpose.

"Right," Alter declared when they'd posed long enough, "Morana: you head off to the laboratory and see if they've come up with anything in their tests on the powder. Meanwhile, I'll scout around the Bailey estate and try and charm my way into his good graces. Meet me there in a few hours?"

"Can't wait," she agreed with a grin.

Death By Chocolate
_____

Two's A Crowd

Alter arrived at Bailey's house and pulled on the bell chord, which gently jangled somewhere on the other side of the heavy oak door.

"Got a nice ring to it," he noted aloud to himself, only mildly disappointed that no one else was about to hear his quip. He had little time to muse on his disappointment as the door quickly opened to reveal the house owner. "Bailey, old chum!" Alter greeted him with a friendly slap on the shoulder. "How are you doing?"

Bailey stared at his visitor for a moment, a strange but misplaced sense of deja-vous filling his head.

"Have we met before?" he asked, perplexed.

"*Have we met before?*" Alter laughed playfully at the apparently foolish question. "Of course we have! I can't believe you don't remember. It feels like only yesterday to me." He smiled to himself and continued with his charade. "It's me; Alter! We had a mutual acquaintance. One, erm… Johnson. Jacob Johnson? He helped you get your first major role!"

Bailey scratched his frowning skull. "That does sound familiar," he mumbled.

"Of course it does, old man," Alter reassured him. "And I was just passing here and thought, I must pop in and see how the Old Bailey's doing, eh!" He laughed jovially at his second pun of the day. Bailey raised his eyebrows in mild-mannered bemusement, but seemed unable to think of a conclusive excuse to rid himself of this unexpected caller. He'd met so many people in his life, and knew so many more who claimed his acquaintance; he was rarely able to remember everyone. Vaguely aware of what he was doing, he found himself inviting the strange man in, hoping the fog in his memory would clear soon enough.

"Excellent," Alter cried as he barged through the doorway before Bailey might have a chance to change his mind. "Is that the kettle whistling to me?" He chuckled to himself again, pleased with his own wittiness, and Bailey closed the door behind them…

⌛

Meanwhile, in a laboratory somewhere in England, not to far from St George's Hospital in fact, Morana was wandering through rows of worktops covered in specimen jars and petri-dishes, surrounded by various workers, busying themselves with the art of science. She kept her head down, trying to look as inconspicuous in her newly acquired white lab-coat as she could, but despite her nerves she went unnoticed. Making the most of this invisibility, she prised open a filing cabinet and pulled out a buff coloured file, marked

'BAILEY, W', musing prosaically at how often buff was the preferred colour for folders, while green was often used for hanging files...

She stopped anxiously as a fellow lab-worker squeezed past the open drawer and her. As soon as he had passed, she flipped through the contents of the extracted file, reading small portions with a frown. Slipping one page out of its comfortable place among its fellow papers, she returned the rest to the cabinet, before tiptoeing out as fast as she could furtively manage...

⌛

Back at Wilfred Bailey Jr's house, Alter had made himself more than comfortable on the green leather sofa, sipping his tea like an English gentleman, joking merrily with his new best friend who was happy to play along, the company doing him far more good than he'd expected it to. The familiar jangling of the doorbell suddenly shattered their new intimacy.

"Ah," Alter announced, returning his cup and saucer to the table, "that'll be my... er... friend, Morana. I asked her to meet me here. You don't mind if I...?" He excused himself from Bailey's living room before the man could argue, walking calmly away until he was out of Bailey's eye-line, and then making a swift beeline for the door.

Morana waited patiently on the other side, looking about her. She remembered the barren fields from her last visit here, though they were now much improved with a pleasant touch of sun upon them. Alter opened the door, stepped through and confidentially closed it to behind him.

"Well? Did you find out anything?"

Morana beckoned him further away from the door, lest Bailey hear their confab from spying behind it. This entire experience was turning them both into highly suspicious spirits - in Alter's case, tenfold-more than he had been before. He leant into his accomplice expectantly.

"Very little, I'm afraid," she whispered in his ear and he stepped back with irritated disappointment.

"Why are we being so secretive then?"

Morana shrugged and Alter shook his head impatiently at her.

"What about the powder?" he probed.

"Ahh, well," she said a little more animatedly, "according to my sources, that appears to be dust."

"Dust?" he repeated with disbelief and they both looked around them in case his raised voice had been overheard.

"Dust," she confirmed. "Just dust."

"What, common old house dust?"

"Not quite." Morana reached into an invisible pocket somewhere on her dress, and pulled out the sheet of paper she had previously borrowed from the laboratory file, showing it to the demon. "Common old *space* dust," she explained as he perused the sheet. "There's nothing remotely amazing about it, and yet there's no earthly way it could possibly have been acquired by anyone on earth."

"How could the old man have got it then?"

"Therein lies the mystery," she replied enigmatically.

"*Still*?" he whined unhappily.

"Afraid so."

"Damn it," he cursed, screwing the piece of paper up in his frustrated fist.

"How about you? How's the acting going?" she asked, looking back towards the converted chapel.

"I am perfect for this part," he proclaimed. "He's convinced we're the firmest of friends and I've managed to talk him into inviting us to a party this evening." He wiggled his fingers suggestively before her, giving a more than clear indication of just how that convincing occurred. She grimaced at him, as ever unimpressed by his underhand tricks.

"Do you really think it was appropriate to put the idea of a party into his head?" she objected.

"Oh, that was entirely his idea, I had nothing to do with it. He was planning it when I arrived," Alter only half lied.

"Really?"

"I swear on his life!" he maintained. Morana crossed her arms and raised an eyebrow at his distasteful suggestion, which secretly pleased him no end. "Well, what would you do with less than a week to live?" He looked at Morana and realised he had doubtless asked the wrong person. "And a party is an excellent way for us - or one of us, at least - to gain his confidence," he added in an attempt to redeem himself.

Morana reluctantly consented and they started to make their way back to the house. Just before they reached the front step, she stopped the demon, pulling him back by his arm.

"Hang on. How is this going to work?" she asked, a new realisation occurring to her. "I mean, it's all very well us doing the investigating and whatnot together, but we are still in competition with each other, aren't we? How do we decide when that starts?"

"Good point," agreed Alter. "We need to decide on rules." He rubbed his chin thoughtfully. "The way I see it, you've got four days left until you're officially revoked, and if I were you I'd quit now."

Morana returned to her unimpressed, cross-armed stance of defiance. "Or?"

"Or," he thought again, "by my reckoning he has about four days left of that dust to drink, even if I am beginning to doubt that even matters. This makes it sound more and more like a placebo."

"Like grains of sand from an egg timer," Morana mused.

"This is not the time for poetry, petal," he patronised. "This is serious." She screwed her face up, but couldn't find the words to argue. "How about we split the four days between us - you have one, I'll have one, you have the next, and so on, giving us an even chance to influence him in our own special ways?"

Morana considered this for a moment before even her brain managed to find the fatal flaw. "That won't work. Whoever gets the last day could have the biggest impact!"

"Damn you for noticing that!" he cursed, although he was secretly pleased. Her ability to spot these things was greatly improved from when they had first met. "OK, fine. We'll take one day each, starting tomorrow, then spend the remaining time competing together."

"Sounds appalling!" she disputed. "But it's the best idea you've had..." She sighed heavily. "Fine. Who goes first?"

"Toss for it?" he suggested, producing a coin. She nodded reluctantly. "I'm assuming you're heads and I'm tails again?"

"Naturally," she agreed.

Alter spun the coin high in the air and let it land on the back of his right hand, covering it quickly with the left. Morana watched him carefully for any signs of cheating as he lifted his hand off to reveal the winner.

"Lucky old you," he grinned, slipping the coin back into his pocket.

"So, what does that mean?" Morana asked, not entirely sure she should feel pleased. "I get tomorrow?"

"Thems the rules," he said, cocking his head like the real winner of the toss.

"Do you already know what you're going to do or say to win him over?" she questioned him suspiciously.

"I think so," he answered optimistically. "All I really have to do is show him how great his life's been so far - thanks to *my* side's influences. Why would he want to stop the fun there?" Morana looked down gloomily at her silver shoes, glistening in the steadily dimming sunlight. "What's the matter? Nervous? I suppose you'll show him his life and point out what a terrible person he was, thus making him feel so much better about his impending doom?"

"Well, I-" Morana began to protest, but Alter was ahead of her.

"Never mind," he interrupted. "I'd better make my excuses with my new pal Bailey. We have a party to get ready for!"

The Parties

Bailey's house was barely recognisable, covered in a cloth of decadence - large quantities of miniature food, loud music; stick-thin, classically beautiful women wearing sparkling dresses, decorated with extravagant beads and chains, their faces masked with thick layers of make-up; men in designer suits and casuals, and occasionally a jot or two of make up on their own skins. Bailey stood in the centre of the appealing crowds, faking interest with amiable small-talk, but appearing to enjoy himself nonetheless.

Morana and Alter arrived, fashionably late on Alter's instructions (even though they'd been sat outside long enough to watch most of the guests' entrances). The front door was opened by an unknown someone, who welcomed them into the revels as if he and his wine glass owned the place. Alter was looking suave and felt instantly at ease with the scene. Morana tried to look cheery, cradling a bottle of wine against her chest.

Bailey excused himself from his immediate company and made his way over to greet them.

"Hey! Alter!" he called out, squeezing his way past partygoers stuck to the walls like flies. "Great to see you again. How long has it been?"

"A few hours?" Alter and Bailey laughed at their private jest, shaking hands like old friends, while Morana smiled uneasily beside them, the bottle weighing down her arms as she waited. Alter intimated his buddy status to Morana, who shrugged indifferently. Their silent communication alerted Bailey to her presence.

"And you've brought your friend from earlier," he spoke to Alter, while looking Morana up and down.

"Morana," she introduced herself, offering her hand to him.

"Morana, welcome," he greeted, taking her hand and kissing it gently, causing her to giggle at such chivalry.

"Um, this is for you," she stuttered, handing over the wine.

"Chateaux Du Papes," he read the label with some bemusement. Alter shrugged apologetically and Morana's embarrassment increased.

"Well, I didn't really know what I should bring," she whimpered.

"No, this is great," Bailey smiled warmly at her. "It's a good year. Thanks. Although you really only needed to bring yourself." Morana giggled again and Alter rolled his eyes at his uninformed companion. Bailey noted the tension between them and decided to add a little festive spirit back into the conversation. "Well, why don't we crack it open and share a glass?" he suggested to Morana. "I'd love to get to know you better."

"Or we could put this on the side with the many others, save it for later, and you and I can continue our conversation from earlier this afternoon," Alter said, feeling his heart quicken at the actor's sudden interest in the angel.

"Well, no offence Alter, but I'd much rather get to know your pretty friend a little better first," Bailey excused himself, beginning to put his arm around Morana's shoulders, but Alter was not so easily dismissed. He artfully stepped between them with a nervous laugh.

"I'm sure you would, but she's not really like that." Morana grimaced at her housemate's attempts to sabotage her.

"What do you mean?" Bailey asked, confused. "You mean she's-?"

"No!" Alter interrupted quickly. "That's not what I mean. What I mean is... Erm... Well it's just that Morana is... She's, erm..." he stammered desperately, trying to think of a suitable excuse, and then noticed the perfect one from the corner of his eye. "Aha! She's a really big fan of cake, and I've just noticed you have an excellent selection here tonight so why don't you, Morana, head over there and take a look and I'll come and join you in just a few moments, OK?" He took the angel's arm and pointed her, not without some force, towards the catering at the far end of the room, speedily diverting Bailey in the opposite direction.

Feeling a little defeated, Morana relented and accepted the call of the food. She picked up a plate and began to pile on the snacks. The array was so compelling, she remained oblivious to the small crowd of women who'd gathered to watch her, nudging each other, slightly disturbed by her enthusiasm.

"That's a very interesting look you've got going," one of the women called over, a hint of unkindness to her observation. "I had no idea until tonight that the chubby cherub look was still in fashion!" A few of the women nearest her sniggered behind their perfectly-manicured hands.

"Thank you!" Morana smiled proudly, pleased to be suitably recognised. Not expecting such an oblivious response, the spokeswoman walked away with a haughty toss of her shiny hair. Alter, who had watched the entire display with a mixture of emotions, tapped Morana on the shoulder.

"Did you hear?!" she asked him excitedly. Alter shook his head with pity.

"She was taking the piss," he explained.

"I don't know what that means," she dismissed him indignantly.

"Do you want me to show you?" he goaded.

"No," she replied despondently, annoyed at how insensitive Alter could be when she least needed it. She turned back to her plate and began to nibble at the little crudités she had collected.

"Enjoying yourself?" he asked, changing the subject.

"S'alright," she shrugged. She looked about her and realised for the first time that she was the only one digging into the display of food. "Why have all this food here if none of them are going to eat it?"

"For the same reason they put stars in the sky that none of this lot will ever reach." He looked at her puzzled face. "It looks good," he illuminated.

"Oh." She considered his analogy for a moment, but decided not to scrutinize it further at this time. Something else had been bothering her. "And what did you mean by *I'm not really like that*?"

"Someone's full of questions tonight," Alter deflected, but Morana could plainly see through him.

"Well?" she persisted.

"Just trust me," he sighed, "you're not." She looked hard at him, feeling anything but trust and waiting for a far better answer than that. "Look, that man is standing on the edge of life and death, which, as you and I both know, is not an easy thing to do. He's throwing a party to distract himself, and, if I know Man, he's thinking there's one sure fire thing that can momentarily help him forget his woes and make him feel pretty good about himself. So believe me when I tell you, you are not it." As he finished his explanation, his gaze was instantly taken up by a passing beauty. "She, on the other hand, is perfect," he salivated, tracking her seesaw hips as they crossed the room.

Morana followed Alter's line of sight to the highly coiffeured model, sipping her cocktail provocatively. Alter had clearly caught her eye too, and she was trapped by his desires. Morana was about to protest at what she suspected was another of his mind games, when she almost choked at what happened next. From just behind the woman, having somehow hidden perfectly within her shape until now, another demon appeared. As she watched, this new demon began to signal with eyes and hands in her direction. She frowned uncomfortably before realising it was to the adjacent Alter that he was referring, and the two were now silently communicating to each other, making a deal for the woman. Terms having been agreed, the tempter demon whispered into the crystal-studded ears, and Morana watched helplessly as the woman, almost in a daze, crossed the floor towards a poor, unsuspecting Bailey, nothing but seduction on her mind.

"I can't believe you two just did that!" The angel turned on her competitor, highly disturbed at how easily the woman had been coerced.

"What?" Alter dismissed her. "She's drunk! She won't remember a thing by tomorrow."

"That doesn't make it right!" Morana yelled in disgust.

"Of course it doesn't," Alter patronisingly agreed. He looked at the angel and shook his head with disappointment. "You know, sometimes I think you forget what it is I do." His accusation was correct; she did forget. She chose to forget, hoping above hope that his actions were down to centuries-old peer pressure rather than his own design. But there were times, horrible times like this one, when she was forced to face a different truth.

"I don't think I like this party," she sulked aloud.

"Why?" he asked, his mind already elsewhere. "Too crowded for you?" Even as he spoke, Morana's jaw dropped, and a mini cheese ball slipped from her tilting plate. From behind and to the side of every human in the room, demons, previously unnoticed, magically appeared, whispering suggestively, furtively beckoning to each other, disappearing and reappearing, until Morana felt sick with claustrophobia. "Yep," Alter rubbed his hands together with glee, "it's going to be one *hell* of a night!" He laughed at his own witticism, slapping Morana on the back and causing a few more cocktail sticks to plummet to the carpet. She squatted down to retrieve the food, and, raising herself back up, returned the half-eaten plate to the table, dejectedly. "Cheer up, Chubby," he grinned at her. "If you start to feel out of place, you can always go and join your lot upstairs?" Alter suggested. Morana looked up at the first-floor balcony curiously, but saw no one there she recognised. "And again," Alter added, lifting her chin helpfully up to the ceiling beams. She still saw nothing, but there came a flash of realisation through her mind.

By the time she lowered her eyes, Alter had already walked off towards Bailey, leaving her to her sombre thoughts. She wanted to be able to stand this for the sake of the competition, but her good grace was rapidly leaving her, and the demonic glares and sly human looks were eating away at her already low self-esteem. Escape was very much on her mind as she surveyed the room for any signs of good. Only one beacon of hope remained as she caught sight of Bailey, watching her from the other side of the room, smiling sympathetically. Her heart jumped at the connection and she smiled back, but her view and those positive vibes were instantly blocked by Alter, once more commandeering the actor for himself.

Bailey was initially as disappointed by this as Morana. He had been admiring the new addition to his party, the way she wasn't afraid to eat the food like all those anorexic acquaintances about him. Her obvious fear of being out of place echoed how he felt inside, and he found himself strangely drawn to watching her, longing for an opportunity to speak with her, and wondering why Alter was so protective of her. He saw Morana looking toward the ceiling, as if wishing she could fly away from the party. Then his view was blocked by a passing group of revellers, making their way noisily to the punchbowl and throwing their appreciative greetings in his general direction. He searched around and between their bodies, but by the time a clear view returned, Morana was gone. He scoured the room, but she had seemingly vanished.

"Bailey!" Alter's voice cut through the host's disappointment. The demon waited for Bailey's full attention to return to him, snapping his fingers surreptitiously to hurry the process along. "Anyway, as I was saying, this is..." he turned to introduce the same attractive woman he had previously bargained for, and her demon whispered the missing information into his ear. "...Sharon," he announced. "And I think you two will get along perfectly, because Sharon absolutely loves you. Although, right now Sharon absolutely loves anyone, don't you Sharon?" he joked flirtingly with her, making his subject giggle ridiculously as she leant vulnerably into him for support. "Exactly," Alter winked at Bailey, unhooking her arm from his and re-hooking it around Bailey's neck. "I also think you'd get on rather well with another friend of hers. Let me just see if I can find her for you..."

Up On The Rooftops

High above the party, a few dozen angels squatted and lolled about the roof tiles, moon-bathing, chatting quietly, or playing Happy Families to pass the time. Morana politely tiptoed about the peaceful congregation, spotting someone she knew lying on the sloped altar roof, looking up at the stars.

"Hello Laniel," she greeted him, smiling down with relief at an honest, friendly face.

"Morana! Come and join me," he motioned beside him. She quickly laid down and gazed at the same beautiful view he had just been admiring. "Look at that," he pointed up to the sky. "Beautiful, isn't it. Why do you think they bother creating something as beautiful as that for a species that never appreciates it?"

"I don't know," she sighed with a mixture of awe and sadness. "Some of them do appreciate it."

"But *we'd* be singing its praises all the time," Laniel affirmed.

"True."

"And what about clouds!" he continued his lecture.

"What about clouds?" Morana frowned.

"Beautiful things! No two cloud formations are ever the same. And yet do *they* appreciate that? No! The minute a cloud appears in the sky, they start moaning-"

"What is going on up here?" Morana interrupted, hoping to avoid a rant. It was somewhat hard to understand why all the angels were sat on the roof, complaining and avoiding everything that was going on just below them. "I thought you were a Protector Angel?"

Laniel nodded his head and motioned towards the rest of the group about them. "We all are," he confirmed.

"Then shouldn't you all be down there protecting? That place is swarming with demons!"

"We know," he concurred solemnly. "Look," he added, guiltily catching her curious glare, "if there's one time our good counsel and protection is never wanted, it's at a party like this. They just refuse to hear us. It's easier to wait near by until the realisation hits them. And then the tears start-"

"Which one's Wilfred Bailey Junior's protector?"

"Mmm? Oh. Well..." Laniel frowned. "I thought that was now you?"

Morana looked at him, perplexed, yet ever so slightly afraid. "No. Not that I'm aware. No, I'm still an angel of death."

"Are you?" Laniel pulled a face that suggested otherwise, but he chose not to argue matters he didn't understand. "Oh. Well, in that case it must still be Raymond. And he's not here."

"Where would he be if he's not here?"

"Back in the Heavens somewhere?" he answered inconclusively.

"I need to find him," Morana determined aloud. Raymond should have been there in Peru with Bailey and the strange old man. Finally, she realised, she might be able to obtain some answers from a first-hand witness.

Protection

For the second time in as many days, Morana found herself outside the back gates of Heaven, without invitation and with no sure idea of what she was hoping to achieve. Just outside the gates, a male cherub sat, singing to himself in a clear, merry voice. She greeted him with a wave.

"Yaron!"

"Hello Morana," he answered, cutting off his song mid-verse. "You're looking very tidy. Suits you." Morana looked down and realised she was still dressed in her party outfit.

"Thanks," she blushed. "What are you doing out here?"

"Oh. Avoiding things," he explained enigmatically, then smiled at her worried frown. "There's not a lot of joy in the choir at the moment. It's very hard, you know, only having one proper gig in two thousand years. If another Christmas goes by and we're not called for..." he shook his head fretfully, "well, I don't know what'll happen. Personally, I'm thinking of putting in for a transfer."

"No! Really?" Morana exclaimed, only half surprised. "What will you do?"

"Actually I really fancy applying to be an echo, you know, at one of those mountainside shrines or something. I'm very good at mimicry."

"Really?"

Yaron opened his mouth and repeated the word exactly as she had spoken it.

"Wow," she said. "That is impressive."

"Thanks. I know," he agreed.

"But a mountainside shrine?" she asked uncertainly. Yaron had always struck her as a bit of an exhibitionist - she couldn't quite place him hiding away amongst the rocks.

"Well, anything's better than waiting around here at the moment."

"I had noticed a little twitchiness lately," Morana pried, hoping that an understanding of his problem might lead her to some answers of her own.

"Oh, if you think it's bad here, you should hear what they're saying about Hell!"

"What?" Morana asked, her spine tickling with anticipation.

"Well, you know how in the great End Days plan they're supposed to start before us?" Yaron confided, leaning in closer to her. "They're convinced we're deliberately refusing to tell them when it'll happen, leaving it until the last minute, so they'll have no time to prepare!"

"You mean they're not already?!" If she'd had this conversation three weeks ago, Morana might have considered Yaron no better than a gossip. But after everything that had been happening, any inkling of a mystery between the two sides was worth following up. "Wow. Things are really going to get bad."

"At least we'll be safe up here, eh?" Yaron beamed positively. "It'll be a good time to be an angel for once."

"Yeah," Morana agreed uncomfortably, in light of her recent decisions. "Erm… If you happen to hear that things are likely to kick off in, say, the next century, could you let me know?"

"'Course I will, love," he laughed, assuming she was joking, despite her serious tone. "What brings you here anyway? I heard you were on special assignment?"

"Oh really?" Morana thought about this for a moment. She hadn't heard it called that before. "Well, I suppose it is. A bit," she conceded. "And that's why I'm here - to visit the Protector Angel Raymond."

"Really?" Yaron looked at her as if he wanted to say more, but decided against it. "You want me to let you in then?" he smiled, pulling out a set of beautiful gold keys.

"If you wouldn't mind?"

"'Course not." He wandered over to the grand gates and clicked the lock back, opening the gate just a crack to allow her to slip through easily. "Only good luck with Raymond, mind. He's been in a strange mood lately, so I've heard."

"Thanks for the warning," she smiled gratefully. "And good luck with Christmas."

"Cheers love," he waved after her as she disappeared through the gates. "Peace be with you and all that."

⌛

A short way into the lower echelons of Heaven, Morana nearly collided with the angel Hannah, who turned to meet her with a look of surprise.

"Hello, what are you doing here?"

"Everyone keeps asking me that lately. I'm starting to get paranoid," Morana answered.

"Don't be silly!" Hannah laughed gaily. "We just thought you'd be busy on your special assignment, that's all."

"Everyone keeps saying that too!" Morana exclaimed uneasily.

"What?"

"That I'm on some special assignment!"

"Well, I'll understand if you're not allowed to talk about it," Hannah tapped her nose and winked secretively at Morana before starting to walk away.

"Wait!" Morana called quickly after her. Hannah turned back with a patient smile. "You're a healing angel, aren't you?"

"Yes?" Hannah agreed inquisitively.

Morana thought for a moment about what she was going to ask, what kind of trouble she might cause if this was wrong, but she had to start finding some real answers. "Do you know someone who could get me... space dust?" she posed.

To her surprise, Hannah wasn't the least bit disturbed by her question. "Anyone could get you space dust," she shrugged. "Surely you could if you-"

"Not just the ordinary stuff," Morana interrupted, her confidence growing with Hannah's positive reaction. "I mean the kind of space dust that... prolongs life?"

Hannah looked hard at Morana, who swallowed slowly, convinced she had said too much. Her friend frowned, then scratched her head.

"Well. Now you've got me," she replied. "I didn't even know there was such a thing," Hannah laughed it off, and Morana relaxed.

"So you've never used it in your healing?"

"No," Hannah replied with a fair amount of certainty. "Can't think of anyone who has!"

"But could it be possible to use space dust to prolong life?" Morana pushed.

"Ordinary space dust?" Hannah pulled an unlikely face. "I don't think so. No, of course not. I'm quite sure we would know by now if it had healing properties of any kind. But if you're asking me if it *could* be used..." she scratched her cheek thoughtfully, "well, I suppose if you wanted to use something symbolically physical, it is possible. But it would have to be blessed. And I can only think of about four beings in existence who could effectively do that."

"Thank you," Morana smiled and walked away from her friend, satisfied for the first time since the mystery began.

⏳

It took a few wrong turns, and numerous directions from myriad angels, but eventually she found herself outside the door of the workplace within which she had been informed she would find Bailey's Protector Angel, Raymond. She knocked on the door, but there was no response. Listening closely, she heard the sounds of turning paper, clinking glass, scratching pen nibs. Someone was definitely inside. She took a deep breath and slowly pushed the door open.

"Hello?" she called out as she stepped into the small room. She found herself staring at the back of a male angel, dark curly hair covering his head, which was half-bowed over the table before him, directing all its energy on the work below. He did not turn to acknowledge her, nor complain about the intrusion. "Are you the Protector Angel Raymond?" she asked tentatively. The man paused briefly at the sound of his own name, but still refused to leave his work and greet her. "My name is Morana, Ang-"

"I know who you are," he snapped irritably. He spun around to look at her and seemed momentarily surprised at the sight before him. She again remembered she was not really dressed for such an occasion, and apologised with her eyes. "Are you here to gloat?" he growled.

"Gloat?" Morana straightened with surprise. "No. About what?"

"About taking my job from me! Without a moment's experience."

"But I came here to ask you..."

He turned his back on her as she spoke. Morana sighed heavily. His reaction was not quite as she had envisioned and was sending her back to the same hopeless feeling she had felt before the deal with Alter. "Look, there seems to have been some kind of confusion. I am an angel of death. I've come here to ask you why you've given up protecting Wilfred Bailey Junior?"

"Given up?" he rounded on her. "I gave up nothing! He was *given* to *you*."

"But I'm an angel of death, and he's still alive!"

He watched her desperate protest and for a moment was almost moved to help. But his honour had been slighted.

"That's no longer my problem," he dismissed her.

"Of course it is!" she cried. "He's down there, right now, surrounded by a bevy of demons, not a good thought in sight." She looked at him with pleading eyes but his face was like stone. "And, like you say," she added, appealing to his dignity, "I don't have a moment's experience of protecting. I'm bad enough at death!" she half-joked, while Raymond's scowl suggested he did not find this in the least bit amusing. "He needs you now more than ever. And I won't believe for a moment that you don't care."

Raymond looked at her, waiting to see if she was planning to add anything further, pretending to be unmoved by any of her words.

"If you've finished, I have to read up on my next assignment," he coldly concluded.

"That can wait a couple more days, can't it?"

Emma Walker

Morana's Day

7 AM in the housemates' kitchen. Alter sauntered in, yawning widely, searching for a mid-sleep snack. Even before he reached the refrigerator his mind was beginning to tick. Something was waking him up. Something other than hunger.

The kitchen, he realised, was unusually tidy for the time of day. Not just tidy, in fact; spotless. And within its domain, at 7 AM in the morning, stood the Angel Morana, fully attired in a white summer dress, neat of appearance, and most definitely awake.

"Morning," Alter stretched sleepily, checking the time on the wall clock suspiciously. "You're up early," he confirmed.

"Today's my day, isn't it," she replied confidently. "With Bailey."

The photograph, with its fake black moustache, pointed beard and glasses, smiled smoothly from the fridge door, taunting Alter's lack of preparation.

"What's going on? You look like you know something. I thought we were working together on this?"

"Not for the next two days, remember?" Morana couldn't hide her smiles.

"Fine." Alter glared at her, annoyed by her confidence, but too tired to argue. He reached into the fridge and pulled out a large slice of cold pizza, smothered in thick cheese and multiple meat pieces. His mood instantly changed as he reappeared from behind the door. "You missed a cracking party last night," he grinned, ripping a huge mouthful away from its triangular existence and munching noisily on the fabricated squares and balls of pig and cow parts.

Morana slinked across the kitchen and stopped dead right next to him. "I'm glad," she whispered into his ear, smiling enigmatically. He paused in his chewing, seething at his food as she disappeared from the room and made her way out of the house.

⌛

Bailey's driveway was littered with taxis clearing away the remaining carcasses of the previous night's orgies. Morana waved with friendly smiles, and greeted those departing with a "good morning". They responded with grunts at best, but most simply ignored her, presuming her to be a domestic worker of sorts, there to clean up their devastation, and not worthy of their patronage. Morana was unfazed by their attitudes. She gazed nosily into the back window of a passing car to see a woman she vaguely recognised as the beauty Alter had admired the night before. But that same beauty had faded with the hours, and her once sparkling eyes now looked vacant and mildly confused.

The front door was open, but Morana still knocked politely. At the end of the short hallway, Bailey's head appeared around the wall. His hair was dishevelled and a few tired, grey lines had appeared below his eyes, but he was still apparently bright of spirit, and he smiled excitedly at her appearance.

"Morana! Come in," he beckoned with one hand, then disappeared back around the corner. She did as he suggested, closing the front door behind her. Bailey smiled again as she joined him in the kitchen. "Last of them's finally gone," he intimated to the window and the trail of dust and crunching gravel from the last departing taxi. Morana nodded. "I never thought I'd be able to cope with a morning after again. Apologies for the mess," he added, this time motioning towards the living room behind her. "The cleaners will be along later."

"That's fine," she smiled politely, choosing not to look, more interested in the small spoonful of powder he was adding to his freshly poured drink. "What's that?" She asked innocently. "Some sort of powdered milk?"

He looked nervously down at his now wet and empty spoon. The packet of powder was sat open on the kitchen counter and he covered it up poorly with his palm.

"This? Erm... No. Not exactly." He picked the packet up and stuffed it quickly back inside the statue of an Inca god. "Sorry, how rude of me, I should offer you a coffee," he apologised in an attempt to change the subject, but her steady gaze was making him burn with the need to confess. "No, it's... erm... a sort of pick me up thing," he mumbled, pushing the sealed statue as far back on the counter as possible. "Not drugs!" he added, suddenly realising how it might look. "It's just something I picked up in a recent trip to Peru. I'd let you have some, only there's not much left." He poured out a second cup of coffee and offered it to her.

"It's fine," she said, gratefully accepting. "I don't know what it would do to me anyway," she mumbled into her first gulp. Bailey appeared not to notice her loose comment. He was more interested in ushering her away from the scene of his guilt and into the living room, mess or no mess. He swept some of the debris of books, pictures, forgotten clothing and plates of uneaten food, off of the sofa and they sat down together. There was a moment's silence while they sipped their coffees, smiling uncertainly at each other over the mug rims.

"So, how're you feeling this morning?" he asked, impressed at how fresh she looked for the time of day.

"A little tired," she answered. "I don't remember sleeping at all last night."

"You and me both!" he laughed, then suddenly felt embarrassed by the implication. "So, what happened to you last night?" he deflected. "I looked around for you, but you'd disappeared early on. Did you get lucky?" The moment the words were out of his mouth he felt foolish, though he couldn't explain why.

"I'm always lucky," she remarked innocently, and he assumed she was playing along.

"I think you and I have a lot in common," he winked.

"I don't know," she frowned uncertainly and his apprehension returned.

"Sorry, no, you're right. I just... I do feel... There's something, isn't there?" He stumbled weakly over his explanation. "About you. I feel like I should be honest with you." He laughed at his own foolish feelings.

"I hope you are," she agreed with a straight face. Something pricked him all over. Morana was the strangest woman he had ever met. He was used to women submitting to his charms in a relatively easy fashion. He was also no stranger to those women who liked to try and play it cool, hoping to hold his attention a little longer than the last had. But Morana aroused feelings in him he simply couldn't explain. She wasn't a classic beauty, yet she glowed with an indescribable radiance. Her innocence, such as it appeared to be, was charming, while it seemed to belie a greater wisdom, which made him feel like a child in her presence.

"So, what do you have planned for us today?" he asked hopefully.

"Erm... Nothing," she admitted, and panicked inside. She had made plans, yes, but she hadn't thought to plan something special for the two of them. A nice chat was as far as she'd got. But now he was looking at her with those expectant eyes, and she knew this was the bit at which Alter excelled. All she had to offer him was the truth.

"Nothing? Really?" Bailey responded more with surprise than disappointment. "I was under the impression from Alter that you were going to show me a good time?"

Morana smothered her scowl within her cup as she deliberately took another sip and pondered on just how much sabotage Alter had already managed.

"Oh," she gargled, lowering her cup to her knees. "Well, I had hoped we'd have a nice time together, of course, but I really hadn't planned..."

Bailey laughed kindly at her discomfort. "Well, not to worry," he reassured her, trying to decide if she was being genuine or playing a very clever game. While he pondered on this, Morana's attention was distracted by a hissing sound from somewhere just behind her. She half-turned to see Raymond, partially visible between the long curtains, pointing excitedly at a small display shelf just above her head. She shrugged with her brows and Raymond rolled his eyes, stretched out his arm and tapped at a photo frame, which fell with a clatter into Morana's lap, causing both her and Bailey to jump.

"Sorry," she reacted instinctively, catching Bailey's bemused look. "I don't think I touched it."

"Sometimes I think this place is haunted," he mused as she turned the frame over to view its contents.

"Who is this?" Morana asked, not feeling nosy, but sensing this was part of Raymond's plan. She allowed her fingers to follow the outline of the young, uniformed man in the picture, smiling back at her with bright composure.

"My brother."

"I didn't know you had a brother?" She remarked with surprise.

"Really? You've not read my websites, fanzines and unauthorised biographies, then?" He half-joked. Changing tone he added, "I don't talk about him much."

"Why not?" She asked, allowing him to take the picture from her.

"He died," he replied with a rehearsed composure. "More than ten years ago."

"I'm sorry," she said genuinely. "And he was a soldier?"

"RAF actually," he answered, a moment's pride flickering across his face. "Yes, my brother did everything just right. Worked his way up the ranks. Made my family very proud, while I was busy fighting for attention on stage and screen." There was a hint of sibling rivalry to his voice, enveloped in lonely sadness. She sensed he had secretly enjoyed the battle for their parents' approval. Without his brother, the battle had lost its verve. "I had a psychiatrist once who tried to blame all my bad habits on my family." He looked deeply through the glass and into the glossy-paper eyes. "But he was never not there for me, my brother, and more than once he bailed me out of a tricky spot. Here was I, the brother with all the money, anything I wanted, swimming pools, fast cars..." Bailey sighed sadly. "I never had half as much as him. He had the family and the respect. Sometimes I think it's a cruel world that allows a hopeless case like me to continue living, while a good and brave man like my brother..." He looked up at Morana and saw the sympathy in her eyes. He shook his head with a feeble laugh. "How's that for self-pity?"

"Everything has its reason," Morana smiled kindly. "Especially death. You'd be surprised how often tragedy leads to something positive." Bailey smiled back but she sensed he didn't quite believe her, and she was beginning to wonder why Raymond had thought that talking about this was a good idea. The atmosphere was growing positively morose. "How about a walk?" She suggested in an upbeat tone as he replaced the photo on the shelf. "I've noticed a lot of footpaths down the way? We could have a picnic?" She felt excited by her spur of the moment decisions and was a little taken aback at Bailey's sudden hysterical laughter.

"Oh, you're serious," he said and stopped laughing just as suddenly, sorry for the discouraged look in her eye.

⌛

Their walk took them along a narrow country road, cutting through local farmland. The sun was shining ahead of them. The trees swayed with a pleasant breeze, which echoed through the grasses. Birds sang, butterflies fluttered about the weed flowers, and everything seemed peaceful, idyllic, just as it should...

And yet, Morana could not escape the feeling that something was following them, slinking its way through the grass and trees, disappearing from sight whenever she turned to look. Even Bailey was affected by a sense of foreboding.

"I'd be quite happy to go back for the car?" He suggested nervously. "It's a convertible," he added, hoping to seal the deal with the promise of fresh air within his comfort zone.

"No, no. I'm fine, thanks," she lied. "It's so beautiful here. Very peaceful." She took a deep breath, and allowed herself to be distracted by nature and the wonder of creation. The wind whipped through her hair and the sun gently warmed her face. "It's moments like these that are the reason I stay here." She followed the flight of a black bird as it dived within the branches of a large, old tree and froze.

"Stay where?" Bailey asked. Morana could not take her eyes from the tree. Bailey followed her hard stare, but could not follow her reason for it.

Alter waved casually at her through the leaves, posing artfully on top of a thick branch. A broad smile stretched from ear to ear as he intimated to something further down the path.

"Oh no. This is all I need," Bailey groaned aloud.

"What?" Morana span her attention around to him in alarm, terrified of what might be to come.

"Down there," Bailey pointed along the road where, a little way in the distance, Morana spotted the broken down car and the two young women hovering around it. She immediately sensed a trap.

"We can take another path down if you like? Cut through the field?"

Much to her dismay, Bailey sighed with only feigned disappointment. "No, that's okay," he said, beginning to make his way towards the damsels in distress. Morana looked back and saw Alter smiling down mischievously.

"Really, there is another path. I saw it, just down the hill there." She could feel herself tensing as she pleaded with him, but Bailey's mind was already made up.

"No, no. They might need our help, I suppose."

She was beginning to strongly dislike this pretend reluctance of his, but she could see she had no choice.

"Well, if they need our help..." she relented, trading spiteful glares with the enemy...

The females had managed to lift the car's bonnet, but were making little attempt to do anything else beyond standing around, foolishly waiting for an even more foolish male to attend to them. The weather may well have been clement for the time of year, but it was all Morana could do to stop herself from making negative and unfair judgments about their ridiculous choice of attire; shorts that took their name to the extreme, and tops that may as well not have been worn for all the good they were doing to cover their plentiful assets. Morana took a deep, calming breath, while Bailey sauntered over to them, hands in pockets, a contrived nonchalance to his posture. Morana tottered up behind him, but she may as well have made herself invisible for all the attention they gave her. In fact, there were moments when she wondered if they could see her at all, and she was tempted to raise her wings in protest - that, she told herself, would certainly get their attention! At least it might, but she couldn't be sure...

"Bonjour monsieur. Pouvez-vous nous aider?" One of the women called out as Bailey made his approach.

"Sorry, ladies, my French is a little limited," he smiled fawningly. "Do you need some help?" He gestured to the car, and Morana rolled her eyes disdainfully.

"Oh, you are English," the woman gushed. "Yes, do help, please." The two women stepped to the side and allowed Bailey an uninterrupted view of the car's engine. He rubbed his hands together and leant over the hulking metal coils and boxes.

"Hmm," he mused as Morana looked over his shoulder.

"You could just call out a mechanic for them?" she suggested as Bailey scratched his head.

"Hmm? Oh. Yes. Morana," he spoke her name as if he too had forgotten she'd been there until now, "that's a good idea."

A good idea it may well have been, but the young women were not so impressed, causing Morana to suspect their English was just as good as their French was bad. They were not at all happy to see Bailey talking to her so intimately and sidled in closer to the actor, pretending to check the state of the engine themselves. Probably for the first time that day, the angel speculated. Bailey smiled all round and pulled out his mobile phone with the same sense of power that a knight might have felt at unsheathing his sword in days gone by. He scrolled through the long list of numbers he never used until he found a suitable name, then pressed to make the call. He smiled reassuringly as he placed the phone to his ear and listened. After a few quiet seconds, he lowered the phone and looked at it. Then he shook it a few times and listened to its earpiece again. Then he moved his arm wildly about, making a few spins around the car, looking for all the world like a very bad disco dancer.

"No signal!" he frowned. "That's rather odd. We can't be more than a mile from my house..."

"We are having this problem too," the second woman announced conspiratorially. Morana looked about her suspiciously.

"Are you Wilfred Bailey?" The first woman asked hesitantly.

"Ah, yes, I am," he replied with embarrassed pride, shuffling his feet modestly, but looking up slyly through his flopping fringe to watch as the women screeched and jabbered frantically to each other at the sight of their idol. A few moments into their adulation, Bailey's crafty peeking fell on to the less than impressed and slightly anxious face of Morana, and a pang of guilt brought him back down to earth.

"I don't suppose you have any knowledge of cars?" he asked, wandering over to her side.

"Not exactly," she admitted in a voice that made her sound as if she knew far more than she was letting on. "I think I can fix this though," she announced.

"Really?"

"Yes," she said in a cagey tone. "Can you try the ignition?" she ordered him.

"Sure," he assented, impressed by her newest talent.

Morana waited until he was out of her eye line, and the French women had predictably followed him to the body of the car; then, as he turned the key, she tapped the engine and it started perfectly first time, growling back to life with more gusto than it had ever had. Morana dropped the hood back down as Bailey came to congratulate her. The two women huddled about the actor, heaping on praise in multiple languages. At first he blushed with pride at their attention, but he remembered Morana more quickly this time.

"Ladies, really," he protested, unpeeling himself from their embraces, "it was nothing to do with me. Morana here-"

"But you have the magic touch!" the first woman interrupted.

"It would not start before you tried," the second woman sycophantically agreed.

"And now it is sounding better than ever!" They clapped hands like a couple of excitable children, and, in much the same vein, they turned to each other to share a giggled whisper, which seemed to result in a unanimous decision. "He should come with us," the first woman said aloud.

"Oh yes, you should come," the second confirmed, taking hold of Bailey's fingers. "We are going for a great ride now, perhaps even to the sea!"

"You must come with us!"

"Say you will?"

Morana could barely contain herself. It was like watching a couple of kindergarten children playing with a puppy. And, just like the puppy, Bailey was enjoying every minute of their attention, and doubtless would have rolled over on command too. But Morana underestimated his intelligence. Just as she was beginning to consider the day lost, Bailey's common-sense kicked in. He had wondered about the car breaking down so close to his home, then starting up again so easily with barely a touch from Morana. Now he was being accosted and enticed by two admittedly beautiful young women and, instead of appearing attractive, they were making him feel uncomfortable. Right on cue, Morana coughed politely from just behind him.

"Ladies, I'm flattered, truly. But I have a prior engagement," Bailey said, disentangling himself from their grasps. "Some other time?" Before they could argue, Bailey and Morana walked away together, leaving the women's moans behind them, both angel and actor satisfied at what had just passed, both for their own reasons. The groans of disappointment seemed to mutate the further away they travelled, until Morana could almost hear a devilish wailing in the air. She closed her ears to the sound and forced a smile to her lips. She couldn't see the mirrored grin on Alter's lips as he trailed the trees above them. A bunch of clouds were forming a collective overhead, and a low-pitched rumble made Bailey shiver. Morana stopped dead in the road. Bailey turned to her, a fear churning in the pit of his stomach.

"You know, I've just realised, we've come out all this way for a picnic without any food!" Morana slapped her head foolishly.

"Should we go back?" Bailey asked, a little too eagerly.

"No," she disappointed him. "I think I can see a small garage with a shop just down the way. They may have something edible."

Bailey followed her gaze down the path. There was indeed a distant building, but he could not make it out. "You must have excellent eyesight!" he squinted.

"Mmm, it's pretty good," she answered idly. "Long distance. I'll go and take a look." She started down the road.

"Shall I wait here?" Bailey called after her.

"Oh." She turned back to him. "Well, yes, OK. I'll be quick. You can..." she hesitated, checking the trees and shrubbery and finding it clear of demons, "...admire the scenery?" She smiled casually, hoping he couldn't sense her disquiet. He smiled back, barely reassured, and she restarted her walk towards the distant building, constantly looking over her shoulder to watch for a break in Bailey's view of her. She saw him perch on top of a nearby stile, gripping tightly to the fence panels and, with his attention distracted by his own concerns, she opened her wings and disappeared. Alter looked down at her abandoned charge and smiled a little wider than before.

⌛

Despite her speed, Morana returned to find she had been outmanoeuvred once more, though this time she had at least predicted it would be so. Bailey was stood talking with Alter, looking considerably more relaxed than when she'd left. Beside them, a sports car was inelegantly parked across the road.

"Ah, Morana, we were just talking about you," Alter greeted her slyly. She walked straight over to her competitor, and hissed in his ear.

"What are you doing here?"

"Just passing," he answered nonchalantly, burning with pleasure in the face of her discomposure. "Thought I'd see how you two love-birds were getting on."

"Love-birds?" she repeated with annoyance. "We're getting on fine." She looked back at Bailey and down at the two shop-brought, plastic wrapped sandwiches in her hands. "I think. Don't you have somewhere else to be?" she snapped, forgetting that he didn't.

"Of course!" he lied flamboyantly. "But how could I not stop when I saw my two best friends in the world stranded by the wayside?"

"We're not stranded, we're…" Once again she became very aware of the squidgy bread between her fingers. "We're having a picnic," she finished feebly.

"Really? Without a hamper?" Alter persisted meanly, playing on Bailey's much more affluent lifestyle than two plain sandwiches could satisfy.

"I forgot-" Morana began to explain, but Alter cut her off cruelly.

"Of course you did." He nodded at her handfuls. "But you have brought something along."

"Yes," she answered glumly.

"What?"

Her embarrassment was growing by the second. She knew he shouldn't be making her feel this way, and perhaps he wasn't. Perhaps it was the bewildered stares of Bailey watching their sparring match that was the real cause of her discomfort? The two men were waiting expectantly for her answer.

"One tuna mayonnaise and one ham salad sandwich," she described meekly. "Sorry," she turned apologetically to Bailey, "it was all they had that looked edible. I thought we could share them? Oh, and I have an apple too." She produced the fruit from between the folds of her skirt.

"An apple!" Alter mocked. "How droll. I suppose you intend to share that too?" He shook his head condescendingly at her. "But seriously, if it's lunch you're after," he said, addressing his words to Bailey, "I am in fact on my way to a stunning gourmet. It does the most exquisite seafood platter, Champagne, dessert... It's got to be better than soggy tuna and rubbery ham, hasn't it? Oh, and the apple, let's not forget," he motioned derisively to the fruit before turning back to Bailey. "It's a very private place?"

"It sounds very tempting," Bailey admitted, "but I actually think the sandwich and apple will be fine." He smiled as Morana raised her sad eyes, now colouring over with surprise. She turned to see Alter looking just as shocked as she felt.

"You can go with him if you want to," she told Bailey, not wanting him to feel obligated to her just because she was there.

"No, I really don't," he reassured. "After the excesses of last night, simplicity is just what I need. And you were right about this fresh air too!" He drew a deep cleansing breath and both angel and demon looked at each other uncertainly. "Sorry, Alter. Some other time, perhaps?"

Alter paused, a look of defeat on his face, which for once Morana could not take full delight in, still being somewhat confused by the mortal's reaction herself.

"Well, there's always tomorrow," Alter relented. "You two enjoy your picnic, won't you." He leaned across to Morana as he made his way back to the fancy car. "I'll see you later," he growled in her ear and she replied with a simple smile.

Emma Walker

Review

A few hours later, Alter did indeed see her, walking into the kitchen, where he had sat waiting for her return, a bottle of Bourbon to keep him company. He had imagined her return over and over in his mind; she would walk in with a beaming smile of success, he would slice her head off with a giant bread knife, like a kitchen-show version of Highlander. He didn't fancy having to clean up the mess though - that was usually her job. And he did feel a little bad, considering her head was one of her best parts. He could wait until she slept, then pluck her wings bare? Except that angels didn't sleep with their wings open anymore than demons slept with their tails hanging out of the covers. He pictured her return being smothered in a dull grey mist, her coughing outline barely visible in the doorway. "You've been smoking?" she'd say; "I was feeling anxious," he'd reply, letting another cloud billow out from his armpits and backside, watching her slowly asphyxiate as he cackled wildly...

He had pulled himself together in time for her return, though not without chuckling to himself about his 'smokin' arse'.

"Good day?" he asked, trying very hard to greet her with sensible composure, but the bitter twinge to his tone, coupled with the effects of the Bourbon, gave him away. Morana made no response. She looked neither happy with herself, nor upset by a possible disaster. In fact, she appeared totally expressionless, which was far too disconcerting.

"Not planning to see him again, then?" Alter joked through the tension.

"How could you do that?" she suddenly turned on him.

"What?" he protested with some innocence.

"Cheat!" He rolled his eyes with realisation. "We had a deal - one day each!" She reminded him.

"Hell's teeth!" He shook his head, growing weary of her need to project her own level of trust and honesty onto him. "What did you expect me to do?" Her face dropped and he almost felt bad for disappointing her again. Almost. "Besides, it was nothing compared to what I could have done," he boasted.

"Nothing! You threw him lust, pride, greed-"

"Don't forget envy," Alter interrupted proudly.

"Envy?" She asked, trying to remember why she hadn't spotted that one.

"Yep. Envy," he confirmed.

"When was he envious?"

Alter's face softened a little. "Of you," he explained. "When you fixed the car."

"Really?" Morana had to stop herself from feeling pleased that she'd impressed Bailey so much, angry at being used to entice a sin.

"Speaking of which," Alter added, recalling her accusation of foul play, "when did you pass your mechanics training?"

"That car should not have been there!" she rejected his counter-accusation, though not without realising he had a point.

"Don't come all high and mighty at me with your 'it's not fairs'. I saw you fix that engine with the old invisible touch. What I'm more shocked about is how nobody else noticed you fixing it without so much as looking at a spanner!"

"Serves you right!" she jibed at him. "Besides, you failed. He didn't give into any of the feeble attempts you made."

"Oh, I think he managed one," Alter scoffed.

"No he didn't," she dismissed him. Although, having missed the envy, she was no longer confident that she'd spotted everything. "Which one?" she called his bluff.

"Pity," he announced.

Death By Chocolate

"Pity?" She racked her brains, trying to remember if pity was still a sin. "For what?"

"Oh my dear, stupid little airhead of an angel," he answered, spilling over with all the cultivated venom from his impatient wait for her return. "How do you think I got him to spend time with you, hmm?"

Morana's head drooped. She thought about all those times she'd felt mediocre - even a failure - in Bailey's presence: turning up to a party with a silly bottle of wine, while everyone else had offered champagne, drugs and their bodies (according to Alter); not having a plan for today, and nearly ruining it with a couple of cheap sandwiches and a walk that had been cut short by bad weather. It was easy to see the pity... But, now that she thought about it, that wasn't all she could see.

"That's not true, though," she smiled, perking up at her extended memories. "He couldn't keep his eyes off of me at the party."

"Is that your vanity showing?" he challenged her.

"No," she answered uncertainly. "Anyway, I'm still not sure if pity is a sin. I'm going to have to look that one up." It wouldn't, after all, have been the first time he'd misled her on something.

"You do that," he dismissed her nonchalantly. "In the meantime, I'm getting ready for the next movie marathon." He sauntered over to the fridge and pulled out a large Black Forest gateau, swirling it seductively beneath her nose. "Join me?" he tempted her, leading her into the living room by her predictably desirous stomach. He placed the cake delicately down onto the coffee table, threw himself onto the sofa and kicked his feet up. Morana frowned down at him. He turned on the TV and sounds of sirens and concerned voices escaped the box in a flashing trail of blue light. "Or we could just watch the news?" He smiled.

"You're a very disturbing being sometimes," she complained, watching his hairy bare toes twitching too close to the chocolate shavings.

"Thank you," he winked, producing a fork from nowhere and tapping the empty seat next to him with its prongs. Afraid for the cake's future, she reluctantly sat down beside him, sliding the gateau away from his feet and accepting the fork.

"Shouldn't you be planning your day with Bailey?" She asked as she delved into the creamy coating.

"No need," he answered with his eyes now transfixed on the screen. "Operation Bailey Destruction will be a piece of cake." Alter smiled to himself as Morana's chewing momentarily stopped and she gazed unhappily at the dirtied fork. "The seeds have already been sown. All I have to do is pick up where I left off with you." Alter was absolutely certain there was no way Bailey would have turned down his pretty French girls and gourmet meals if Morana hadn't been there to make him feel bad. "I did warn you it was never going to be that much of a challenge."

"It still might not be as easy as you think," Morana remarked, pricking hungrily at a swelled purple cherry.

"I don't see why not," he dismissed her. "Ooh, unless you're planning on a little sabotage yourself?" He turned to her in mock fear and expectancy. She looked at his fake expression and shook her head.

"What would be the point?" she admitted sullenly, and he turned to the TV with a loud laugh.

"True. Oh, by the way, some of the other Death Demons are throwing me a party tomorrow night, and the good news is, I've had a word and managed to get you on the guest list!" He matched her raised eyebrows with an excited smile, and she really couldn't tell how much of a joke he was making. "You could be our honorary Angel?" he encouraged her with a rather odd enticement. Morana's questioning frown was unmoved.

"Why are they throwing you a party tomorrow night?"

"Well, you know," Alter pretended to be embarrassed to admit to it, "victory and all that. By tomorrow I will have won a very sought-after soul. It turns out, despite how irritating this whole palaver has been, a lot of the lads are pretty envious of me." His pride glowed red around him. "This could be a huge boon for me. Added to the fact that I'll win you as well! The least they could do was throw me a party."

"And invite me?" she questioned, uncomfortable at the reminder of their bet.

"Guest of honour," he smiled greedily.

"But you won't know," she pointed out.

"What?"

"You won't know by tomorrow if you've won his soul. There's still two more days!"

"Really?" he asked slyly, and she sensed he was giving away a little more of his plan. "Oh, Morana, Morana," he pitied her slow intelligence. "Let's just say, the way I play, you're down to your last pawn and my entire army is advancing. And the way you play, you'll probably invite us all in for tea and chocolate cakes before we slice your head off. Do you see?" She stared at him, unable to make any response, which he took as confirmation she did see. "So, are you coming to the party?"

Alter's Day

The following morning, a confident Alter stood before Bailey's house. A gentle breeze blew against his back as he reached for the bell pull.

"You have to promise me!"

"What the hell?!" Alter almost jumped in the air at the unexpected voice. He turned to see a mildly dishevelled Morana stood behind him, wearing clothes she had quite possibly slept in. "Oh," Alter acknowledged her, adding "What?" as he remembered her sudden demand.

"You have to promise me," she repeated. He frowned, not having the slightest idea to what she was referring.

"You're up early," he changed the subject, not sure he wanted an idea.

"I know," she agreed impatiently, "but-"

"Needs must when the Devil drives, eh?" he joked. Morana scowled, tapping her feet and folding her arms moodily. Alter sighed. "Promise what?"

"That you won't do anything... really bad."

"No," he refused. She looked back at him with hurt eyes.

"Bloody hell!" he cursed. "Fine, no," he relented, before adding, "like what?" just to be on the safe side.

"Make him kill someone?" she suggested after some thought.

"Oh, no," he agreed. "I'm not going to do that anyway. It's too obvious. What else?" he asked, starting to enjoy this.

"Stealing?"

"Hmm..." He tapped his chin. "Can't promise. But it isn't on the agenda." As if to confirm this, he handed her a piece of paper which did, indeed, lay out his agenda for the day. "See?"

Morana took it from him sceptically and read through, gradually screwing her face up with each line.

"Oh, some of this is disgraceful!" she objected.

"You disapprove?" he asked with a happy grin.

"Yes!"

"Good." He clapped his hands with self-satisfaction.

"Although it's not as awful as it could have been," she yielded. "And I see you are at least allowing for free will, rather than *making* him do things," she added approvingly.

"It would be unsporting of me if I didn't," he granted. "And he really has no chance either way."

"What's this 'Grand Finale'?" she pointed to the unspecified bottom section of the page.

"Oh, that?" Alter brushed her aside sheepishly. "Nothing. It's just a big surprise. I'm still toying with the details." Before she could question him further, the front door opened and she instinctively whipped the paper behind her back before Bailey should see it.

"I thought I heard voices," Bailey said. "Alter, good to see you. And Morana..." He ran his hand self-consciously through his hair. "I hadn't expected you. Are you joining us today?"

"No she isn't," Alter snapped quickly.

"Oh," Bailey noted disappointedly.

"She's just here to see us off," Alter confirmed.

"OK," Bailey said, sensing what he assumed to be a little more tension in the air between them. "Well... I had a really great time with you yesterday," he told Morana, hoping to keep her talking a little longer, perhaps even change their minds.

"Me too," she agreed, blushing a little. She leaned across towards Alter and whispered "See!" in his ear. The demon waved his fingers before Bailey's face, sending the actor drifting away in a daydream.

"He's lying," Alter turned coldly to her. "Feigned politeness." He snapped his fingers and Bailey blinked as though someone had just shone a bright light in his eyes.

"Sorry, what? I just zoned out there for a bit."

"I was just saying, that sound's like our ride coming," Alter rubbed his hands together as a fancy sports car, not too dissimilar to the one he had brought along the previous day, drove up to the front door. The same two obviously pretty women from yesterday were also present in the front and driving seats.

Morana rolled her eyes disdainfully. "Oh, please."

"I don't believe you've met my two good friends, Candice and Lucie?" Alter introduced the two ladies to Bailey, ignoring Morana's disapproving groans.

"I don't know," Bailey faltered, growing distracted from Morana by the moment. "Although there is something familiar-"

"Yes yes, perhaps you've seen them around," Alter interrupted impatiently. "Well, anyway..." While he began to explain the whys and wherefores of the situation to Bailey, Morana was distracted by the sight of Raymond skulking behind a tree. She backed slowly away from the car scene towards the Protector Angel.

"You're here!" she whispered happily to the tree trunk. "Thank the heavens! Oh, and thanks for yesterday too."

"I did very little yesterday," he demurred.

"I think reminding him of his brother may have had some effect."

"Next to what your evil demon is doing?" he sneered. "We're going to need a miracle to make this one work. And why aren't *you* going with them? If *you* were going, I wouldn't have to go, and besides it's quite obvious he likes you-"

"Stop!" Morana almost yelled too loudly, growing tired of Raymond's protests. "There was so much wrong with that sentence, I don't know where to begin! Alter and I had a deal - one day each. I'm already almost breaking that rule by sending you along." She smiled and waved at Alter's suspicious glances, leaning casually against the tree.

"Almost?!" Raymond unnecessarily griped.

"You have a right - no, a duty - to stay with Bailey while he lives," Morana said, more to convince herself than the unwilling Protector. "And I really need you to, Raymond. This could be the most important thing you ever do for him."

"Oi, Angel!" Alter yelled from the car before Raymond got a chance to argue further. "We're off!"

"Angel?" Bailey questioned Alter. "Is that a nickname?"

"Err... Yes?" Alter excused himself.

"It suits you," Bailey told Morana as she sheepishly arrived at the car's side.

"Thank you," she reddened again.

Bailey and Alter were now sat in the front seats, the girls having been relegated to the tiny spaces in the back. While Morana kept them distracted, Raymond crept up, turned himself transparent, and perched on the back bumper, muttering yet more complaints for Morana's ears only: "Oh, the things I'll have to hear and see today! I thought we were at an end of all that..."

"Shhh!" Morana warned him.

Alter swung his head around suspiciously. "What?"

"Shhh..." Morana panicked a little, pushing Raymond's barely visible apparition down into the boot. "Shhh... ould get going, you should," she fumbled. "Have a nice day."

Alter gave her one last glare of distrust before putting the motor into gear and speeding away; Bailey looked back over his shoulder at Morana as they left, disappointed not to get the chance to say goodbye; and Raymond's head and praying hands stuck out of the boot, his eyes turned up to the sky in miserable desperation...

Death By Chocolate

Morana And Alter Are Recorded In Front Of A Live TV Audience...

Morana spent an anxious day, mostly in front of the TV, eating a variety of sweets to keep her mind off what might be happening to the party in the red sports car. Later that evening, Alter came home and made his way straight to the kitchen. Morana stayed still on the sofa, oblivious to the sounds of clanking bottles, sobbing her heart out at the television show. Alter leant against the living room doorframe, sipping his beer behind her, grimacing at the display of female emotions on the screen.

"Honestly," he scoffed, making Morana jump and rub her eyes dry with her knuckles, "we gave you Jerry Springer, yet still you want to bore yourself with Ricky-fluffy-Lake."

She waved a damp tissue of greeting in his general direction, sniffling. "Sometimes we like to see peaceful resolutions to problems," she reasoned.

"Bloody nonsense," he dismissed irritably, sitting down next to the angel. "And how is it that you can eat so much and still not turn into a cherub?" he asked her, kicking at a nearly empty tub of chocolate-chocolate-chip ice cream on the coffee table. She sobbed a little more loudly at his mockery and Alter rolled his eyes, passing her the tissue box. The TV audience resounded with an approving "Ahhh", applauding as she ripped a tissue free and used it to blow her dampened nose. They moved to a convenient ad break and Morana turned back to Alter.

"So, how did it go today?"

"Pretty good," he answered, taking another slurp of his drink and not giving anything much away.

"Really?"

"Mmm..." he responded dispassionately. "Rough start, of course. For some unfathomable reason, he spent the first ten minutes or so talking about you, which was a real turn off for me and the ladies."

"What ladies?" Morana teased, smiling happily to herself.

"Very funny," he said without humour. "Anyway, things got a bit easier after I found out about your little friend..." Alter was now the smiler, impishly grinning at Morana.

"What? Who?" she asked puzzled, when almost instantly it hit her. "Oh, no! Raymond?"

"Oh yes. Raymond," he mimicked.

"What did you do to him?" she asked in panic.

"Nothing much. Just made sure he stayed out of the way..."

⌛

...Translucent he may well have been to the naked human eye, but Alter had had his suspicions from the start. At the first opportunity, he'd banished Raymond to the inside of the car boot. The reluctant and terrified Protector Angel crouched in a foetal position, while Alter's mini demons danced around him, poking him with their mini pitchforks and jibing cruelly...

⌛

"If you've harmed him..." Morana began to threaten, but Alter stopped her with a finger to her mouth.

"He's fine," he said in a calming voice, freeing her squashed lip. "Probably a little shaken up, but it serves him right for being where he wasn't wanted..."

⌛

...Alter had rather enjoyed driving over as many bumpy country roads as he could find, as fast as he possibly could, while Raymond was tossed about the boot like a pinball in its machine, the mini demons sharing his fate, struggling to keep up their vigil as they flew about the tiny space...

⌛

"What was it you said again about cheating?" Alter asked her pointedly.

"He had every right to be there," she argued.

"Yeah, yeah," he dismissed her. "Either way, it made no difference. Bailey made the most of the day, much as I'd planned, and the Grand Finale, in the end, was better than I could ever have predicted!" He toasted himself with his own beer.

"What did you do?" She glared hard at him.

"I did nothing!" Alter protested his innocence. "Unfortunately, one of the girls mistook his *magic powder* for brown sugar, if you know what I mean?" Morana shook her head and he sighed. "Drugs, Angel! She tried to snort the stuff. Used most of it up and made a bloody mess with the rest."

"Why would she think it was drugs?" Morana asked disbelievingly.

"I don't know..." Alter tried to look blameless, but couldn't quite meet her eyed. "Somebody must have put the idea in her head?" Morana scowled at him and he couldn't resist a smile. "Funny thing was," he continued, as though it really didn't matter, "it did absolutely nothing for her. Didn't even make her feel especially healthy. Don't you think that's funny?" he prompted Morana, whose mouth was gaping, speechless. "Considering how it made Bailey feel? You'd think it might do something? Morana? Don't you think?" He waved his hand in front of her face, which hadn't changed expression throughout his appraisal. The almost forgotten TV audience booed as they waited for her response.

Death By Chocolate

"You've killed him."

"What?" Alter exclaimed, remonstrating

"That powder was the only thing keeping him alive," she slowly reminded him.

"Case in point: how could *I* kill a dying man?"

"He had at least two or three days left."

"Three days of what?" Alter objected. "Sitting around miserably, considering his limited time? There's a reason humans don't get told their date of death beforehand."

"You couldn't wait three days?" she yelled crossly.

"Call me impatient," he agreed calmly.

"You have done some low things since I've known you…"

"Thank you," he accepted her growling accusation.

"…but this?" She shook her head.

"Is exactly what I'm meant to do!" he affirmed. "I'm a demon of death; so are you."

"*Angel* of death!" she corrected him. "I actually care about what happens to souls."

"No you don't," he rebuffed. "That's why you're going through all this - because you left so many souls for me!"

"I didn't leave them for you, you stole them from me," she argued.

"Because you weren't there," he confirmed.

"Not because I didn't care!" she objected.

"You keep telling yourself that," he said pitilessly.

"This is just not like you," she moaned at the offence.

"This is exactly like me!" he retorted. " I know *you* want to believe that I'm a nice being really. That's what makes it so much fun, living and working with you. You're so innocent and forgiving. So easy to manipulate."

"No, it's not true!" she shouted desperately. "I don't care what you say. I know you feel bad about this."

"I feel victorious!" he refuted.

"You left a man in absolute despair!"

"I did my job!" he shrieked back at her, causing her to shrink back miserably into the cushions. "And I did it well," he added in a quieter tone, almost feeling sorry for the pitiful sight before him. He snapped back to his usual self as the audience applauded the end of the segment. "And now I'm off to party." She pouted at him and he passed her the tissue box again. "And so should you. It could be the last chance you get for quite some time." He smiled at her, as though making a kindly comment.

"I want to go and see him," she sniffed.

"Who?"

"Wilfred Bailey Junior!" she whined.

"Why?"

"I want to make sure he's OK."

"He's not." Alter laughed offhandedly. Morana glared angrily at him. "He never has been! And now he's - *what a surprise!* - going to die. How can you possibly make him OK?" Morana looked close to crying and Alter shook his head dolefully at her. "Just leave him. It'll all be over soon."

"I want to tell him the truth," she blurted out.

"What?"

"I want to tell him who we really are and what we've been doing."

"Why?" Alter looked at her with disbelief. "And you think I'm disturbed! He won't believe you."

"Then it won't matter, will it," she reasoned. "Besides, I don't care. Maybe I'm not doing it for him or his belief." Alter smiled approvingly at her sudden selfish desire. "If I'm about to become human-"

"*My* human," he interrupted.

"Then I want a clear conscience. A clean start."

"Ridiculous," he sneered, but she refused to drop her determined look and he saw he had no choice. "You know what? Fine. Go and tell him everything that's happened. It can't do anything but push him deeper into despair and confusion. He's spent his last day realising that sin is highly preferable to that squeaky-clean and frankly boring nonsense you lot push out, so if this is a final attempt to convert him-"

"It's not," she dismissed. "I won't even try. I'll just tell him the truth and go."

Alter raised his eyebrows questioningly. "No staying there until he dies? You tell him, then come straight to the party, yeah?"

"Yes," she agreed to the terms.

"Excellent," he concluded, leaving her to her isolated confusion. "See you there."

The Last Visit

Bailey opened the front door and quietly let Morana in. They sat opposite each other on the sofa. The empty packet, which once held the mysterious powder, was on the table between them, amidst photos, rolled pieces of paper and other strewn mess.

"I'm so sorry," Morana tried to comfort him.

"For what?" he asked forlornly.

"I know," she said, pointing to the dusted plastic bag. "I know that you're dying and that the powder was the only thing keeping you alive."

He blinked at her with surprise. "How?"

"I don't know how," she answered, assuming he was referring to the powder's effects. "I've been trying to find out, but-"

"No," he interrupted, "I mean, how do you know I'm..." He still couldn't quite bring himself to say the word. He'd been fooling himself ever since Peru.

"Because..." she took a deep breath, "I'm an Angel of Death." She waited for the laughter, the jeers and mockery, but in fact he said nothing. "And Alter - he's a Demon of Death." Even this resulted in silence from her audience of one. "We get sent at the first moments of a person's death, to help them through it - through the transition from life to death. One way or another..." She stopped, noticing Bailey was looking down at his lap, seemingly distracted by his own hands. "I know you probably don't believe me," she sighed.

"Actually, I do," he surprised her. "Well, I think I do. I've had a feeling something strange was going on ever since I met you two. I felt as though I'd seen you both some place before. I kept thinking about my appointment at the hospital..." Morana looked down sheepishly at her own lap. "But the memory was all fuzzy. My guess was that you were journalists. But angels of death...?"

"Actually, the whole hospital thing was very perceptive of you. We *were* there," she admitted, "in the doctor's waiting room. We were trying to find out what was wrong with you and what was in the powder."

"But you didn't?" he asked, a tinge of hope to his voice.

"It's a genuine mystery," she disappointed him.

"So, why me?" he asked, having given her confession some thought.

"That's another one."

"Another what?" he asked, confused.

"Mystery," she said. "We really don't know. We - Alter and I - had never been sent to a living person before."

"So you've no idea why you were sent to me?"

"Other than to help you into your death? No," she admitted. "We thought you might be an arguer."

"Am I?" Bailey laughed in bewilderment.

"Not sure," she answered seriously. "It got a bit more complicated than that."

"But I still could be?"

"Technically," she explained, "but I don't think-"

"What would I have to do to become one?" Bailey interrupted.

"Oh. Well... "Morana hesitated. "Alter always does this better than me," she confided. "Erm... Basically, an arguer is someone who doesn't believe in an afterlife, or doesn't want to die yet. Or knows that he'd probably been a bit bad at times in his life, but doesn't want to face a judgement or punishment - if that's what he thinks an afterlife involves." She looked at Bailey's face, hoping he understood. "Something like that."

"OK. Put me down for all three then," he smiled jokingly.

"Oh..." Bailey winked at her uncertain face. "I must say, you're taking this very well," she approved. "Most people refuse to believe, even as they leave their deathbeds and find us right in front of them... Although Alter did say you wouldn't believe me."

"Right now, Morana, if you told me you were an extra-terrestrial who'd just beamed down to borrow a cup of sugar, I'd probably believe you," he justified.

"Oh," she said disappointedly. "I see."

"So what happens next?" he asked, feeling some vague purpose through the gloom.

"Alt... er..." she stopped herself short from telling him the worse of the situation. "One of us comes to collect you."

"And then? I assume I go to heaven or hell?"

"For a bit, yes."

"For a bit?" he repeated, perplexed. "What do you mean?"

Morana pursed her lips uncomfortably. "I probably shouldn't say."

"Will it make a difference?" Bailey probed. "Presumably I'm headed that way fairly soon? Or are you worried you'll get into trouble?"

"No, actually you're right," she said after a thoughtful pause. "It's too late to be worried about that now. OK." She took a deep inhalation and began. "Well, it works like this: a soul dies and then, depending on his beliefs, he gets collected by one of us demons, and taken to the next stage of existence, which could be Heaven, Hell, Valhalla, the Field of Yalu, or preparation for reincarnation. Whatever the soul has spent his life believing in."

"I never realised there were so many choices," Bailey remarked. "Sounds like a cocktail bar!" It was the sort of comment Alter might have been proud of, but she was still pleased not to have been laughed out of his house.

"The choices were always there during your lifetime," she explained. "But you're limited in death, obviously. Or, at least, the first stage of it. And, of course, some people believe themselves worthy of punishment, so that side of their soul has to be satisfied before they can move on."

"So if I don't consider myself punishable for all my bad deeds, then I get away with it? Shoot straight to Heaven?" He asked with amused disbelief.

"Erm, no, it doesn't work that way either," she said. "You might convince yourself that you're above the law - both of the physical world and the spiritual afterlife - but your soul retains a record of everything you do, say, think and feel in life. And the soul is not only linked to your body and your conscience, but also to the Universal Soul, of which we are all a part. So your judgment will come from inside you, but will be the result of all things, not just those actions you thought mattered."

Bailey frowned like a student at the end of a long lecture on a Friday afternoon. "Well then surely everyone goes to Hell, or whatever equivalent they've thought up?"

"Oh no," she argued, "for that very reason, many people who think themselves bad or unworthy discover the complete opposite is true once they reconnect to the Whole. Good and bad are very relative human concepts. You people put a lot of thought into what 'is and isn't' in life. But really, once you die, you realise it didn't matter for the reasons you thought. I have heard," she began to eulogise, "of so many souls complaining that they led a really virtuous life, doing everything by the book and all that. Then they died and found themselves stood next to a neighbour who, in their human opinion, apparently did nothing for anyone while he lived. 'How is this fair?' they all wail." She looked at Bailey, whose expression appeared to be asking the same thing. "So we show them," she smiled.

"Show them what?"

"Their life. What they did. How they helped people or improved the world by their deeds. And suddenly it makes sense to them." She hadn't meant to start explaining it at all, but she was too far in now to simply pull back.

"If you look on life in this world as a temporary placement with no real meaning, or just as a means to an end, then everything you do will seem pointless; everything that happens to you, unfair. You won't care about one piece of dropped litter, one murderous thought, one lie, unless it affects you personally. If, on the other hand, you see the world as a Whole, as something you can make better by your mere presence, with only the tiniest of efforts..." She found herself toying with parables in her head, trying to make sense of the complexly simple.

"So, imagine life in this world, or universe, or however far mankind reaches - imagine it's like being in a garden. Even if all you do in one life is pull out one weed, or sweep a couple of leaves away with your foot, you've made a difference. Hopefully a good one. And your life and the lives that come after you - like other visitors to the garden - will have a more pleasant time because of it. If you have the good of the community at heart when you speak or act, then you'll feel good," she moralised. "You must know what it's like to get that buzz when you've done a good turn?"

Bailey grimaced. "Pride? I thought that was bad?"

"Why can't a man be proud of the results of a good deed?" She contended.

Bailey had no answer. He was mulling over so many new ideas it was making his head hurt. "You said people move on, but where to?"

"I can't say," Morana responded quietly.

"Why not?" he asked, a little annoyed at the sudden withholding of vital information. "I thought you said the secrets of the dead no longer mattered with me?" Morana couldn't remember putting it quite so grandly, but she could understand his frustration.

"Perhaps not," she agreed. "But I can't say because I can't say. I don't know. There are veils protecting higher knowledge from overwhelming us; levels of existence beyond both of our understanding. I'm here in my plane of existence and you're there in yours. Technically, we shouldn't even be able to communicate like this, and yet here we are!"

"Here we are," Bailey repeated thoughtfully. "With me off to Hell any moment now," he half-laughed. "Which I have no doubt I deserve after the life I've led."

"Don't feel too bad about it," Morana soothed. "I'm actually off there myself in a moment."

"Really? You can go there?" He asked, shocked.

"Mmm," she neither agreed nor disagreed. "Well, I shouldn't really. But there are a lot of things that don't seem to matter anymore," she sighed. "And I have been invited to a party."

Bailey wasn't sure how to react to such a remark. Logic had long-since left the building. He wondered if there were hidden cameras or tape recorders about the strange woman, if this was all just a horribly elaborate practical joke, but he couldn't believe her capable of embarrassing him so personally.

"You're such an oddity," he thought aloud. "One moment you're this nice, unassuming, ditsy type - no offence-"

"I-" she began to protest, but he cut her short with his continued theory.

"Running around in the shadows of a guy who... Well, I can't understand how you and Alter ever became companions; you're such a mismatch!"

"Well, we-"

"Then you turn up with this 'Angel-Devil' story-"

"Demon," she corrected, even though he wasn't listening to her.

"Which explains a lot and nothing all at the same time! And you're filled with this ancient wisdom - all philosophising - until I find myself actually believing everything you say!"

"Oh," she wasn't sure whether to be pleased or disappointed by his conclusion.

"I feel like there is so much you can teach me and I want to spend the rest of my life with you, but it would never be an option."

"No," she readily confirmed and found herself thinking back to Alter's past warnings; human interest and emotions could never be trusted.

"What does it all mean?!" he broke through her thought with a frustrated cry.

"I'm sorry," Morana stood, sensing it was time she left the poor man alone, just like Alter had said. "I didn't mean to come here and cause you more anguish."

"More anguish than facing death?" he yelled. "Why should being told that I'm some pawn in a game between heaven and hell cause me anguish?" he scoffed sarcastically. "For god's sake, I don't even believe in all that nonsense! Children's bloody fairy stories. I don't care if you are an angel - you don't even look like an angel," he coldly added, cutting Morana where it hurt. "At least I could believe Alter's a devil-"

"Demon," she corrected him again.

"*Devil*," he repeated doggedly.

"I really don't want to upset you," she said again, trying to calm the mood with a softer voice.

"Where are your wings, eh?" Bailey continued to mock her. "Where's your halo?"

She knew he was going through a difficult time and it was easy to forgive him. She looked down sadly at her feet, realising she was breaking all the rules, every last one of them, with this visit; but she relinquished to his request. Stepping back from the sofa, she sighed heavily, and a white glow began to emanate around her. Bailey sat up a little, watching uncertainly. He nearly jumped out of his skin as two great white wings appeared from her spine and a halo delicately floated above her head. The room lit up spectacularly, and for a moment the angel looked serene and awesome as she drifted lightly before his eyes, but she retained the sad and disillusioned expression, even as he fell back, flabbergasted at the scene. As she reverted to her humanised form, his own temperament turned melancholy.

"I'm sorry," she once more apologised. "I shouldn't even have come. I just wanted to make sure you were OK. And Alter was right, I just made things worse." She looked down at Bailey who remained speechless. "I have to leave you. But... Just don't be afraid."

Hell's Angel

Against her better judgement, Morana tidied herself up, wiped away the gloom of the visit to Bailey's house, and entered the strange bar in which Alter's friends had arranged his party. There were two-tone lights flashing around the ceiling; the usual, highly-favoured red, but she was amazed to see that black lights could actually shine! Only in Hell, she thought to herself, avoiding the questioning eyes that accompanied her entrance. She ducked between flame-lit posts and loud groups of crass demons, pumping and grinding against each other, shouting over the loud music and chinking glasses, until she found a quiet spot at the side of a bar.

Alter appeared before her through a gap in the crowds, sidling across the floor with a slight swagger.

"Hey! You made it," he hugged her. "Nice to see you came in fancy dress," he mocked and she stuck out her tongue making him laugh ridiculously in that way people do at alcohol-imbibing social situations. "Punch?" He ladled them both out a glass from a large, dark crystal bowl. He clinked her glass in an unspecified toast and they drank, she a little more tentatively than his merry downing in one.

"Sweet," she commented.

"And yet slightly bitter," he expanded. "It's great, isn't it?" he grinned. "Reminds me of you in the mornings." Morana scowled at his slurs. "Oh, I'm going to miss those loving looks when you're human. Speaking of which, did you manage to see our - sorry, *your* - lost soul?" He winked.

"Yes," she answered dolefully.

"And was he broken and miserable? Rubbish company, I'll bet. Did he laugh you out of the living room?" he nudged her.

"Not exactly."

Alter looked mildly worried at her response. "Did he believe you?"

"I don't think he knows what to believe now," she said honestly.

"Well, I did warn you that you couldn't help him," Alter dismissed his own concerns.

"I know. It seems you were right."

"Of course!" He toasted the air with an empty glass.

"Well, well," came a recognisable voice from beside them. "If it isn't the odd couple." Morana turned to see Abalam, that same demon she had struggled with in the past, now wearing a quite outrageous black silk shirt, opened far too widely across a hairy chest, to reveal an unnecessary gold medallion. She didn't even want to dwell on the tight leather trousers.

"Hey! It's Abalam!" Alter reached out to his friend for a manly handshake-hug. Morana caught the sly look as he hugged her housemate and she didn't like it one bit. "Nice of you to come, you old devil!"

"Demon," Morana corrected under her breath.

"I wouldn't miss this for the world," Abalam said in a toadying voice. "Well, maybe for the world," he joked, and he and Alter put on their phoney laughs at a jest they had no doubt heard and shared many times before.

"You remember Morana?" Alter continued his greeting.

"How could I forget? Always a pleasure," Abalam turned to her with impish eyes and Morana smiled back uncomfortably. But she was not to be the focus of his real torture that evening. "Celebrating a little too soon, aren't you?" he returned to Alter.

"Well, you know," Alter replied casually. "It's only a matter of hours now, and this lot can party forever." He swung his hands to the room, and those nearest to him cheered at his projected enthusiasm. "We might even go for a ten second countdown."

Abalam leaned into the Angel and Demon with a very satisfied look on his face. "Your soul is already dead," he announced in a theatrical whisper. Right on cue, the music stopped, the laughter and dancing ceased, and the room echoed with the suddenly ominous flickering flames.

"What?" Morana and Alter exclaimed together.

"Dead," Abalam confirmed. "Freshly deceased."

"Oh dear," Morana whimpered, genuinely upset by the news.

Alter looked around the quiet room, the glares of expectancy on the faces of every guest. "Let's get partying then!" he declared exuberantly.

Nobody moved.

"The party's over," Abalam announced. Alter frowned, puzzled.

"Who collected him?" Morana asked quietly, not wishing to attract attention to herself, but unable to avoid it in the current tension, everyone staring at them with increasing intensity.

"That... Should be me...?" Alter said, realising the point she was making.

"It would be you," Abalam agreed, "if you had won his soul. Obviously, you didn't," he grinned smarmily at the demon's continued presence.

"You?" He growled accusingly at Abalam. "You stole my soul at the last moment? You can't do that! He wasn't on your patch - he wasn't on anyone else's patch! He was mine!"

"It wasn't me," Abalam denied. "It seems Wilfred Bailey Junior may have recanted on his death bed. Someone else was there to take him."

Every demon in the room seemed to turn simultaneously towards Morana, who was shrinking back into the shadows, a sickening feeling in the pit of her stomach.

"You?" Alter asked in disbelief. "You? How could you? You stood there pretending everything was fine! How could you betray me? I thought we were friends?"

Somewhere in the room someone snorted a giggle, which set the rest of the room off, until they were all laughing at Alter's foolishness. Morana's fear was overcome by a terrible need to stand up for her demonic friend in a situation she had first-hand experience of.

"I didn't!" she protested feebly. "I swear, when I left him he was alive. He didn't believe me!"

"Well, who could it have been then?" Alter demanded, still condemning her. "You were the last person to see him!"

Angel thought back to her departure from Bailey's house that evening. She couldn't help remembering that shimmer by the curtains in the corner of the room. She had assumed it was just a reflection of the light she had been emanating in her angelic form. But the more she thought about it, the more she noticed the outline of another angel. The outline, in fact, of…

"Raymond?!" she confirmed aloud.

"What?" Alter sneered. But before they had a chance to fight her realisation out, their PDAs bleeped, summoning them individually to urgent meetings.

"Time for you to go, Alter," Abalam smirked.

An angry mob began to encroach upon their space, and both Morana and Alter were forced back against the wall. The angel's terror was perfectly justified, but Alter suddenly remembered who he was, and that he was not prepared to go without a fight. Clawed fingers reached out menacingly toward them.

"No! Leave him alone!" Morana shouted from over Alter's shoulder as talons dug into the demon's skin. "I command you all," she tried to sound brave, "to get away!" Her desperate pleas drew nothing but ridicule and rasping...

And In The End...

As they cowered, Alter protected Morana from the punches and scratches raining down on his spine, while she quietly prayed this moment of their existence would end for both of them...

As if in answer, there was a sudden searing flash of light in Alter's eyes, followed by intense calm and quiet. The attack was over; the demons were gone. In fact, the whole hellish party in the bar had vanished.

A breeze whipped against their clothes as Alter and Morana rose up and looked around. They appeared to be standing on a rocky precipice, so high that the ground below it, even the horizon line, could not be seen. The sky was a murky sunset red, broken in the distance by perfect clouds, shooting out rays of light from somewhere above.

As they stood in wonder, two other beings appeared, walking towards them through the soft mist that now seemed to block any escape; one was a large Elder Demon with an aura of importance, who made Alter whimper on sight; the other was the same

Archangel who had chaired Morana's last judgment. It was the latter who spoke first.

"Morana, come away from the demon please."

Morana sensed the doom in the air. She walked in front of Alter and silently refused to move. She had just witnessed the most unselfish act Alter had ever made - defending her from the attack of his own colleagues, when he could have simply blamed her and allowed them to tear her to shreds. She knew she owed him - and would willingly give him - the same level of protection.

"What's going on?" she called over to the Archangel.

"This doesn't concern us anymore. The demons have their own way of dealing with..." he sighed, "these things."

"What things?" Morana persisted.

"Failure," the Elder Demon roared in a voice that sent shivers down the spines of everyone else present, and rippled the mist about them as if it too was affected by the fear. With great stomps, he charged towards the young angel and pushed her aside to reveal a wretched looking Alter. "This is the end of your existence, demon Alter," he pronounced.

"No, wait!" Morana yelled up at the great hulk, moving herself closer to Alter again. She turned to her own kind pleadingly. "You can't let him do this!"

"Morana, he's a demon," the Archangel called out benevolently. "It's out of my hands."

"No! It isn't!" she protested. "I won't let you do this," she raged at the Elder Demon, determined to hold her own against him, though she shook with a fear she had never felt before. To her surprise, the Elder Demon shrunk back down a foot or two and turned with desperate irritation to the Archangel.

"Your angel is causing me some discomfort," he complained. The Archangel shrugged helplessly. "Remove her, or I will send them both to oblivion."

"You know you are not at liberty to do such a thing," the Archangel dismissed his threat.

"Try and stop me!" the Elder Demon scoffed.

Somewhere in the far distance, the sound of a lone, dolorous bell began to chime. Morana's memory was stirred by the demon's words. "Send them both..." she heard swirling about her brain and around them in the mist, matching the tolls, reminding her of something... The Archangel and the Elder Demon continued to argue each other's roles as she finally recalled the memory.

"Wait!" She called out, raising her arms for peace. They all turned to look at her with a mixture of reactions. "You *really* can't do this," she smiled. "The Demon Alter belongs to me." She lowered her arms and crossed them in front of her chest defensively.

"What mockery is this?" the Elder Demon asked.

"Morana-" the Archangel began to remonstrate, but she would not let him finish.

"No mockery. Alter and I have a pact."

The Archangel sighed with embarrassment. "Pacts with demons are against the rules, Morana. You have been told."

"Maybe so," she agreed, growing in confidence. "But it has been made and it therefore stands."

"I do not have to abide by these foolish games," the impatient Elder Demon growled. "The Demon Alter has failed our Master. Are *you* his master?" he jeered at her.

"Oh come now, there's really no need for this to degenerate into name-calling," the Archangel interjected.

The Elder Demon rounded sharply on his adversary. "Remove your angel!" he snarled. "I give you *both* no more warning."

"Morana?" the Archangel pleaded, extending his hand to her.

"Alter and I agreed: if he won Bailey's soul, I would become mortal and he would own me—"

"Morana!" the Archangel shouted with disapproval.

"But if *I* won Bailey's soul," she continued regardless, "both Alter and I would accept a mortal life."

The Archangel and Elder Demon looked at each other, moved in closer to each other, and began a hushed discourse on this point.

"But technically you didn't win?" Alter whispered from just behind Morana.

"Shut up, will you," she hissed back over her shoulder. "I'm trying to save you! Unless you'd rather cease to exist?"

"Let me understand this," the Elder Demon barked. "You both choose mortality?" They nodded. "You would have me spare this worthless beast and allow him to live on the earth?"

"Ahem, a word again?" the Archangel tapped the Elder Demon on the shoulder and they returned to their muffled deliberation. Alter and Morana stood together, their fingers brushing supportively as they anxiously awaited the announcement on their fate.

"Well, Morana," the Archangel finally turned to her, "it seems you made the right choice after all." Morana brightened with hope.

"We accept the terms of your foolish pact," the Elder Demon continued. Turning to Alter he added pointedly, "But never forget who spared your existence."

"I won't," he muttered, turning to Morana. "I-"

But before he could say another word, the ground shook violently. Beneath their feet, the fragile precipice gave way, great chunks of stone falling heavily downward to the sound of peeling bells; and as Morana and Alter slowly fell, their wings, tails, halos, horns - all remnants of their past existence - floated upwards and away from them, leaving them both naked as the day they were about to be born...

Epilogue

Two fraternal twins floated comfortably in their unwitting mother's womb. They were almost at full term, and beginning to encroach on each other's space. The boy-twin kicked the girl-twin, who crumpled her face up unhappily.

"Ow!" she communicated, turning to her brother "Are those horns?" she waved through the fluid at his head. The boy-twin looked perfectly content at this, two little protrusions just visible on his crown.

"Yep," he conveyed back. "And you forgot your halo."

The baby girl drifted her arms up to her head.

"Ssshh... it!" she groaned in bubbles.

Just as the boy-twin was enjoying his jest, his sister's embryonic sac suddenly began to drain rather rapidly. "Oh god, no! I hate this bit!" A large hand reached in around her and within seconds she was gone. For just a moment, the boy-twin looked disappointed and alone. But not for long, as the hand returned to drag him out of his comfortable space.

"Uh-Oh..." he gulped.

Two babies, newborn and still bloody, screamed as the doctor held them aloft, to the satisfaction of everyone in the room but them...

⏳

Thirty years later, Morana sat in a church vestry. Service notes decorated a notice board above her desk. She was dressed in her black robe and dog collar. Her large, gilt-edged bible was sat open before her. She was smiling proudly as she cut out a newspaper clipping - a black and white picture of her successful brother Alter, who was stood in front of a presentation screen displaying positive figures in the form of a bar chart. The headline above him read: "Apple Bites Back Thanks To New Managing Chairman"...

⏳

Alter stood before that same chart, in his grand boardroom, chairing a meeting and addressing the table with gusto.

"...It worked for us in the past, and it's going to save us in the future." His audience clapped appreciatively. Alter accepted their obsequious applause like gold dust as he sat down at the head of the table. The closest attendee slid across a newspaper clipping showing Morana, smiling as she leant against a computer, beneath the headline: "World's Most Popular Vicar says Stay PC".

Alter grimaced with annoyance and started to screw the paper up. But, while the other meeting members were distracted, he unfolded the clipping, picked up a black biro and scribbled a halo above her head. He smiled with mischievous satisfaction. Then, just to be sure, he added a moustache, sitting back to admire his work...

⏳

...Just as Morana herself was doing, back at her simple desk, now that Alter's picture was annotated with a black moustache and horns on his head. She pinned the scribble in pride of place on her notice board, and walked happily away...

⏳

Meanwhile, somewhere in the highest level of the known echelons of existence, the eldest of all guardians returned from his short vacation in the jungles of Peru, looked down upon creation, and sighed contentedly at his work as he gave the globe a spin...

Death By Chocolate

Deleted Scenes

Morana and Alter were, as usual, sat opposite each other at the kitchen table. Two scraped plates, which once held large pieces of Death by Chocolate cake, rested before them; but, despite feeling replete, they were distracted by an animated argument.

"But that's nonsense!" Morana protested.

"Look, I'm just saying, death is the worse thing you lot ever created," Alter asserted. "You should have stuck to the original plan."

"Well, we would have done if you lot hadn't decided to get involved," Morana responded, crossing her arms defensively with a scowl.

"Yeah, yeah, here we go. Blame us because you can't accept that you made a mistake."

"Oh... Pfft!" Morana stuck her tongue out. "Anyway, if you take out death, then you can't have procreation, and if you take out procreation, then you can't have-" she leant across the table and whispered, "- sex."

Alter thought about this for a moment. A world without sex, compared to a world with death, was definitely the less inspiring of the two. "I'm not saying that it's a *bad* thing - from my point of view it isn't." Morana frowned, trying to decide which 'thing' he meant this time. "I'm just saying, nobody likes death," he confirmed.

Morana shrugged. The argument would never be won. It was, after all, far from the first time the subject had been broached. From underneath the table, Alter produced a DVD case.

"Texas Chainsaw Massacre tonight?" he asked with a teasing smile.

"OK," she agreed with only a vague interest. They slid their chairs back across the kitchen floor and made their way to the living room; Alter virtually skipping, as though he had just won the keys to the Kingdom, Morana skulking dejectedly towards the light switch before clicking it off.

⧗

A short while later, the darkness was punctuated by a bright square of light. Morana stood humming a cheerful jazz tune, drowning out the screams and motors from the other room as she perused the virtually empty fridge. She quickly extracted a large slice of chocolate cake, allowed her teeth to slide over its crumbly brown sponge, letting her tongue flick against its creamy butter icing, before enveloping a morsel of it between her lips, her mouth smiling satisfactorily. She licked her fingertips, closed the fridge door with a swing of her hips, and returned the world to darkness.

v